LONELY PEOPLE

FORTY-ONE STORIES

PORTRAIT OF AMERICA, VOL. I

by G. Lowell Tollefson

Lonely People © 2002 George Lowell Tollefson

ISBN-13: 978-0692326817 (LLT Press)
ISBN-10: 0692326812

All rights reserved. No part of this book may be reproduced by any mechanical, photographic, or electronic process, or in the form of a phonographic recording; nor may it be stored in a retrieval system, transmitted or otherwise copied for public or private use (other than for "fair use" as brief quotations embodied in articles and reviews) without prior written permission.

Published by LLT Press, Eagle Nest, New Mexico

LLTPress.EagleNest@gmail.com

In memory of my mother, Eunice Evans Tollefson, and to my wife, Loretta Miles Tollefson

Preface

Why a collection of short stories? Why are they written the way they are? These are questions I would like to answer because they ask how I, as a writer, approach the manner in which human beings live their lives.

Most importantly, I should begin by saying that I de-emphasize plot. I could then follow this statement by offering the defense that other writers have done a similar thing. However, it is what *I* do that is at issue here, and why I do it is what I hope to make clear.

Since most of the stories in this collection do not rely upon plot development, the question of their principle of organization must inevitably arise. For it would be common sense to assume that there should be some kind of a plan governing their structure. Obviously, a story without structure would not be a story at all. In fact, it would be little more than a cluster of words, somewhat like a spaghetti dinner without a plate to give it form and contain its wandering elements. But there is a plan here: I write what I refer to as *visual form narrative*.

Each story is designed to be experienced as a unified and balanced composition, much as a painting would be experienced. Hence the term, visual form. I admit comparing stories to paintings seems rather odd, since a story is extended through time by means of action, rather than in space, as a painting is. A painting is static, easily taken in at a glance, while a story must, according to its time oriented nature, travel away from its point of origin, soon to move outside a reader's field of vision. That is to say, a story extends itself through time and a goodly stretch of your memory until much of it lies outside your capacity to see all parts of it at once. You cannot examine its components simultaneously as they relate to one another.

But this problem is solved by a simple device: brevity. Brevity allows the full content of a story to be held in the mind within a single, observable, narrative frame, the parts of it to be viewed together at your leisure and discretion, as a painting would be viewed. Within limits, therefore, and in most but not all cases, the greater the brevity, the better.

With this purpose in mind, I make a point of choosing a significant dramatic moment, or a thematically related series of moments, often omitting preliminary and subsequent events. Thus the story might begin at the heart of a conflict, or perhaps in the hour of changing awareness on the part of one protagonist or more. Having gotten you, the reader, seriously involved in the situation, I then close the narration.

But suspense is not my purpose here. I do not disregard the denouement. Rather, I omit most everything else, while nothing important is left out. For in visual form narrative all parts of a story must contribute equally and simultaneously to the whole, no one part distracting the reader's attention by taking precedence over another. Therefore, not even a *sequence* of actions should press its significance unduly upon the mind.

Once a story is read and considered, the overall effect of it should arise from any point of view taken by the reader. In other words, whatever character action you may choose to rest your thoughts upon, all the other parts of the story will serve to undergird and emphasize it. It would be like looking at a painting from different angles, focusing upon selected objects. All the other elements within it would then form a supporting background.

*   *   *

To clarify my meaning, it might be best if I state it in terms of my view of human nature, since I conceive of a story as an instrument uniquely suited for revealing our innermost character and experience.

A good fiction writer must certainly know something about human beings. How else is he to create believable characters? Yet each writer concentrates upon certain aspects of human nature of particular interest to himself.

The subtle working of will is my special concern, and in pursuit of it, I have learned that human awareness possesses an inexhaustible richness of texture. Its relation to will is complex, too complex to be fathomed by a simple cause and effect overview of the progress of emotion and reason. This is especially true if one is attempting to understand their bearing upon motivation.

What do I mean? I mean that, insofar as a story is concerned, human nature cannot be adequately understood in terms of plot development. The reason for this is that the latter necessitates a cause and effect relationship between the parts of a story. It demands from the characters in a story a confrontation, which must work itself out into some sort of resolution. This resolution necessarily follows the confrontation, as though one led inexorably to the other.

Say a person hits an obstacle in his daily progress towards whatever material bliss, moral ideal, or escape from discomfort and danger he hopes to attain. That obstacle might be another person, a

iii

principle, or a thing. Upon being confronted with it, he is then required to find his way through or around it, which he generally does by the end of a conventional story. But is life really as simple as we might wish it to seem when we immerse ourselves in the adventures of a plotted work of fiction?

It seems to me that it is not. What almost always takes place is something else. At any waking moment, the human mind is filled with a subtle blend of bits of memory, ideas, prejudices, present experiences, the very scent of the air. These, by their number and complexity, mitigate against any sort of strictly logical pattern in a decision making process. The mind becomes a shifting kaleidoscope of impressions instead, in which rational thought is only one of the participants. Thus our actions may not, and generally do not, proceed from thought alone.

I grant that upon the surface of individual introspection, and in any decision, or series of decisions, which may follow from it, there is an appearance of intellectual clarity, which might resemble the causal relations of a plot. The rational mind presents us with a chain of logic linking our decisions and actions firmly to the physical world. But it is an illusion rather than an accurate representation of what occurs.

We would like to believe we use this reasoning alone to get to our goals. To shore up the illusion, we seek to rationalize our acts while they are being committed, or even afterwards. This is how a large part of the appearance of reason is actually put into place. For it does us good to think we are deliberative creatures. But, for the most part, we are not. We are intuitive, which often makes us vague and unpredictable, not in the least to ourselves.

To put it another, simpler way, let me say this: When we want to determine *how* to shoot an arrow at a target, reason is the dominant faculty we employ. But when we decide *whether* to do so, reason plays a much more attenuated role. All the while we seem to be deliberating, we are, in fact, feeling our way to a decision.

This underlying intuitiveness may be accounted for, I believe, by the aforementioned mix of impulses, both as some of them come together in the conscious mind and as others emerge undetected from its unconscious depths. It is a complexity, a gathering of subtle pressures upon our will, which is far too minute for a direct causal analysis, too faintly shaded to the observing eye for a purely logical exposition.

* * *

Such a view of human nature does not support the rational structure of a plot. Instead it implies that human acts emerge within a complex and subtle milieu of feeling and impulse. No one feeling or impulse necessarily precedes another in its power to move the human will. They act together and thus must be considered together as a means for understanding human motivation.

In other words, all parts of a story written to reflect this situation should be of equal weight or importance to the impression made by the story. That is how the stories in this collection ought to be read.

Lowell Tollefson

June 12, 2002

v

LONELY PEOPLE

FORTY-ONE STORIES

PORTRAIT OF AMERICA, VOL. I

by G. Lowell Tollefson

Contents

Rear Guard

By October of 1950, United Nations forces had pushed the North Korean army northward to the Chinese border. In November of this same year, Chinese troops crossed the Yalu River, joining forces with the North Koreans. The UN offensive was shattered, the Eighth Army in disarray, the Tenth Corps broken apart. Seven Chinese infantry divisions surrounded the U.S. First Marine Division as it began a bitter, fourteen day fight across eighty frozen miles to the sea and evacuation from the port of Hungnam.

Baker Company from the First Battalion of the Fifth Marine Regiment had spent almost the whole night digging trenches and foxholes along a low ridge line surmounting a gradual incline which sloped into a deep valley. They were to act as part of a flanking defense for a continuous flow of vehicles and weapons on a road not far to their east. In fact, it was just the other side of the ridge.

In the very early hours of the morning, after settling into their newly prepared fighting positions, the men of Baker Company had undergone a heavy barrage from Chinese artillery. Miraculously, they hadn't taken any casualties. Chinese gunners, unaware of their position, they thought, had been interested in disrupting the flow of troops and traffic on the road. It appeared some rounds—a good many, to be sure—had simply fallen short of the target.

Morning broke. The first light revealed a sterile gray, overcast sky. The ridge line, devoid of trees, looked out upon a brown, treeless landscape broken up into hills and hidden valleys. A light snow was falling.

"Can't see anything out there," Private First Class Joseph Eaton said.

"Maybe they're not there," Thomas Walker answered. He was crouched down in their foxhole, trying to spoon the last contents of his open can of rations into his mouth.

"Is that all you ever do is eat?"

"I don't plan on starving." Private Walker had his gloves on. He partially unzipped his heavy parka and pushed his hands under its warm lining. "Damn it's cold!"

"They have to be out there somewhere, man."

"Maybe. But they don't know we're up here. They might want to hit the column later, further to the south."

"No. It's quiet. There hasn't been anything for more than two hours. It's eerie. I don't like it."

Behind them a sergeant was moving toward them in a crouched position. He stopped beside the trench to their right. The trench contained four men. They had a Browning automatic rifle. A young Marine appeared to be having a problem with the seating of the magazine or the loading of the weapon. The sergeant hopped into the trench and helped him. He was carrying a green canvas satchel slung over his left shoulder. It looked like a mail pouch, but he pulled grenades from it and distributed them among the four men. Eaton and Walker watched.

"What's he doing?"

"Handing out grenades."

"We got all we need."

"Not if they're out there."

The sergeant began pointing to a ridge in front of him. It was higher than the one they were on and sloped off into a low range of hills to the left but continued unbroken to the right. The sergeant explained something to the four men, then crawled out of the trench and came over to the foxhole.

"Morning, Sarge."

"You saw what I was doing?" He was handing out the grenades. Several to both men. As he spoke, he was looking out to where the ridge in front of them broke into the line of smaller hills.

"Reconnaissance came upon a mess of them last night. As much as maybe a regiment. Probably more by now. They're behind that ridge."

"Was that before the shelling?" Walker asked.

"Before and during. The patrol made contact, then withdrew."

"I didn't hear anything," Eaton said.

"That's because of the barrage. You were probably in the bottom of this hole cleaning out your drawers."

"Maybe." Eaton smiled.

"So what's keeping them?" Walker asked.

"Nothing. They're just letting you get nervous."

The snow had begun to fall heavily. It was so thick the opposing ridge line was almost invisible, appearing here and there through the snow in small patches. A sharp wind caught the snow and swirled it over their heads, stinging their eyes and cheeks.

"Damn! I can't see anything," Eaton said. There was panic in his voice.

"Neither can they, if they try to come now," Walker said. He had stuffed the extra grenades into the pockets of his parka, picking up a can opener he'd dropped and putting it also into his pocket.

"Goddamnit!" Eaton said. His voice shook. The sergeant had moved off and disappeared to their left. There was no trench to their left, but a foxhole with two men in it fifty feet away. "I wonder if Martin and Peterson are getting the word."

"I think I see the sergeant over there."

"Where? I don't see anything."

"Here they come!"

"What?" Eaton grabbed his M1 rifle and leaned forward, squinting into the snow beside Walker, who already had his weapon in his shoulder and his finger on the trigger, moving the barrel to the left of the ridge in front of him. "Damn! You sure? I don't see anything at all." Eaton's arms were shaking from cold and fear. He was trying to sight align his weapon, bracing it for steadiness on the hard packed, icy ground in front of the foxhole.

A heavy gust of wind turned the snow from a northerly drift and sent it whirling southward. Behind the movement of wind and in the pocket of still air that followed it, both men could see the Chinese soldiers in white uniforms moving through a defile between the hills just south of the ridge in front of them. The Chinese quickly fanned out in a line, the steep rise of the valley to their backs and the gentler slope of the lower ridge before them. They started running toward the Marines waiting above. A Chinese bugle rang out faintly through the wind and snow. Not a shot had yet been fired. Below and behind Baker Company, on the road to their east, just beyond their ridge, the main body of the First Marine Division continued its orderly southeastward evacuation of men, weapons and supplies.

Lonely People

It was one of the old hotels along Third Avenue in Seattle. Not more than five stories tall, it is no longer there now, and even then it was only a hotel in the sense of having a lobby and rooms for rent by the day, week or month. It was a fire trap. Such places burned to the ground often. Their inhabitants, from an unofficial societal viewpoint, were expendable as well. That is why it was all eventually torn down and the whole area given a face lift of newer, expensive, more fashionable buildings.

Terence McCarthy rolled over in bed. He was naked, twisted in the bed sheet, his upper body and one leg exposed, the other leg beneath the wound sheet. It was ten o'clock in the morning, a weekday. He had a splitting headache, the kind that starts behind the eyebrows and goes all the way to the back of the head, taking off the top of it. A harsh beam of light, entering the dark room around one end of a bent, dusty set of window blinds, did not help matters. He turned his face to the opposite wall, then, frustrated, let out a moan and sat up. He thought the sheets smelled musty or moldy. But it wasn't the sheets. It was the mattress.

Terence's head began to swim. The room spun around. Where the light beam coming from the blinds struck the white paint of the opposite wall, the paint was yellow from generations of smokers. He fell back onto the bed and slept until noon.

At one in the afternoon Terence was in his favorite restaurant. It was inexpensive, undecorated, merely functional, down in a basement near Pine Street. There was a piano and a bar. But no one ever played the piano. The bar didn't open until later.

"What'll it be, honey?" The waitress stood next to the plain white booth where he sat. She was blond, a woman in her late thirties, wearing a short skirt.

"Breakfast, sweetheart," he answered acidly. "You still got the breakfast on?" He was twelve or thirteen years younger than the waitress and did not like being referred to condescendingly as "honey."

"Sure," she said. "What'll it be?" She smiled.

Terence, who still had a headache, looked at her knees. Her legs were thin, the knees a bit knobby. Not that she was bad looking. She just had that worn, experienced look one often finds in such waitresses. An appearance of too many late nights, cigarettes and alcohol. Like himself, he thought.

"The hot cakes with one fried egg." He paused. "And coffee."

The waitress went away and returned shortly with a hot cup of black coffee.

Terence had his head in his hands, his elbows on the table, his fingers dug into his black hair, disheveling it.

"Here's your coffee, honey."

"Stop calling me honey!" Terence looked up. "I'm sorry. I've got a headache this morning."

The waitress smiled. Terence observed that her narrow, thin lipped face was modestly pretty when she smiled. "That's okay," she said. "I understand."

"Understand?" Terence's head was back in his hands.

"Sure. I've had a few too many lots of times. You know, I've got something that'll fix you right up." She went off and came back in a few minutes with a small tumbler filled with what appeared to be tomato juice. Terence hadn't touched his coffee. "Here, try this. It'll clear your head," she said kindly.

Terence picked up the glass without looking at the waitress. It was cold, sweating on the outside. He turned it up and emptied it in several gulps.

"Wow!" he gasped. "What'd you put in that stuff?"

"A little lemon, salt, pepper and Tabasco sauce. It'll clear your head."

"More like to blow my brains out."

"It won't hurt you."

"How do you know? You ever tried it yourself?"

"Many times. I think your hot cakes are ready." She went off.

Terence drank his coffee to cool his throat. It was hot too, in a different way.

When the waitress came back with his breakfast, Terence could honestly say he was feeling better. He asked the waitress to sit down for a minute. There were no other customers in the restaurant, so she did.

"Where'd you learn to make that stuff?" he asked.

"Been so long I hardly remember. Works, doesn't it?"

"Must be eighty proof."

The waitress laughed. "No, that's what you had last night, honey."

Terence looked at her in silence for a moment. She had slender wrists and hands and a narrow waist. There was a trace of freckles across her nose. She had too much mascara and eye liner on. "You're cute," he said.

The waitress looked down.

"Don't mean to be forward. I've noticed you here before. You're new."

"Yeah, I used to work over at the Tin Drum. You know. The place near the Pike Street Market."

"I was there once. Too noisy. The music's too loud. I don't remember seeing you there."

"It was probably my night off." She grinned, looking at him. "I got canned for not letting one of the customers fondle me."

"They fired you for that?"

"Yeah. Well, I protested kind of loud."

They both laughed.

"What do you do?" she asked.

"Nothing. I've been laid off from Boeing for the last four months."

"It's tough all around," she said looking at her nails. Terence could see they were chewed.

"When do you get off?"

"Six." She looked into his eyes, as if trying to determine his character. "Girls like me get hurt easily sometimes," she said.

"I don't want to hurt you."

"I know." She grinned, then got up from the table. "You better eat those hot cakes. They must be cold by now." She started to move away.

He touched her arm. "Six?" he asked.

"Okay," she said.

Young People

The round faced harbor seals were not more than fifty yards from shore. It was the first time he'd seen them there. The water of Puget Sound was choppy, and they bobbed brown speckled among the whitecaps, among the green waves that swelled under them and broke over them and crashed into the thin strip of gray sand beach. Behind the beach here and there, a hundred, two hundred yards toward the tree line, were houses, large, expensive, multistoried homes of modern architectural design, made of natural wood and full of glass.

"Never seen them this far inland before," he said. His arm was around a girl, and they were standing together in the wind on the beach. The wind blew a steady stream of salt spray into their faces, raised their hair and pressed their jackets against their bodies. Nevertheless, it was neither wind nor salt that had brought tears to the girl's eyes.

"They look cold," she said simply.

The boy, though older than the girl, was not more than seventeen himself. The full weight of his young manhood was upon him, for they were there to figure out a response to the consequences of what they had done. "Come on," he said.

They turned and walked up the dirt road leading from the beach toward the houses. There were puddles in the road from the last rain. To their left was a bog of brown, stagnant waters covered with white scum. Along its bank beside the road grew a thick green tangle of Oregon Crab Apple, cherry and other small trees. The crab apples were past their white flowering, just beginning to set fruit, producing tiny, oval offspring. But neither the youth nor the girl, who came there often, cared to notice them now.

"I could quit school," the boy said. He paused. "Otherwise we'd have to wait another year and a half."

The girl did not answer.

The youth, who was holding the girl very close, his arm around her waist, could feel her small body. She was warm, sweet to be held. He was sure he loved her very much, though he felt he hardly knew her. He tried to imagine what it would be like to be married to her for ten or twenty years.

"I told my mother," the girl said, her voice barely audible.

"What?" The wind was blowing very hard. It made a roaring sound in the trees beside them and swept in over sand and estuary to the right of the road.

"I told my mother last night."

"About us?" The wind was deafening.

"Yes."

"What?"

"Yes. I told them I was pregnant."

They came to a bend in the road, where the road curved to the right and led up to a densely forested cliff top above. Most of the houses were just below this cliff, though a few were at its summit, perched near the edge but tucked in among trees, some of whose roots grew out and hung down the side of the cliff. The trees were all evergreen, principally Sitka Spruce and Western Hemlock, tall, dark, swaying and creaking in the wind under a low gray sky. Behind the youth and girl, the sun was setting west of Puget Sound. It sank over the Pacific Ocean, salmon colored and magenta in a screen of mist and clouds. Spray rose and drifted like steam over the churning water of the Sound. A few shearwaters turned sharply in the air, their underbellies shining white in the available light as they reeled and dove from the sky.

The two young people turned left onto a narrow path. The ground was muddy, and they had to pick their way among boulders and a large tree trunk that had fallen in the recent rains from the cliff above. The cliff was now on their right. On their left was the tree lined bog, which ended some thirty or forty feet short of the cliff. They could smell its brackish water. It was much quieter along this path.

"What did your mother say?" the boy asked.

"She said she was afraid this might happen, that she knew we were getting too serious." The girl added quickly, "She won't let me have an abortion either."

The boy thought about this without answering. He was uncomfortable with the idea of an abortion. It seemed too dangerous, or cold, or unpleasant, or something. He wasn't sure. But he knew the pregnancy wasn't the girl's fault alone. It was as much his fault as hers.

They came out of the path onto a gravelly shore. Here and there among the rocks were red alder and willow seedlings. But these plants never got a chance to mature because they were in the primary flood plain of the Elwha River. Forty feet away, the river cut through its banks like a pair of jaws, rushing down to get a grip on the ocean. The river and ocean were like wrestlers. From where they stood, the boy and girl could see their waters grappling. Silt rose from the river bed and churned in thick currents below the surface. In their smooth, supple struggle, the river and incoming ocean fought like strong, naked men.

The youth and girl stood along the rocky river bank in wordless admiration. A flock of gray and white herring gulls was gathered on a yellow sandbar in the river. Several of them rose and wheeled above the little island. When they landed, others took their place. Occasionally, a salmon or trout would break water and flash silver into the air. But it always seemed the fish was back in the water before they could turn to see it. Then another would break from the opposite direction.

The air began to grow dark, but the boy and girl did not move. They stood rooted in silence, contemplating the place where they'd first shared love. It had been wonderful then. The youth was sure this was where the girl had conceived his child, though they'd been together elsewhere at other times. The thought of his seed developing in the girl made the young man feel older than he was used to thinking himself.

The young woman sat down on the rocks and pulled the boy down beside her. "I love you," she said, drawing close to him.

"I'm sorry," he said. "For what's happened. I love you too."

The darkness increased and settled into night about them. The moon came up and, searching the black river like a flashlight, found them still sitting together on the moon whitened stones, frightened and alone.

Scotch and Soda

The young woman sat on the bar stool and crossed her legs. She wore high heels and a short, black, cocktail dress with a low neckline. She adjusted the hem of her dress at her knees, smoothing the light, summer fabric over her legs. They were very good legs. She was drinking a whisky and soda because she could not bring herself to guzzle beer like several of the men and one or two women.

"Hello," the man sitting next to her said, raising his glass and drinking from it. He was looking directly at her. She saw him in the mirror behind the bar before she glanced over toward him.

"Hello," the young woman answered softly.

"I don't believe I've seen you here before," the man commented. He set his glass down with a clink and pushed it across the bar, indicating his need for a refill. The woman observed that his arm was strong, for he had his suit jacket off and was wearing short sleeves. His hand was large, pale but lightly calloused, obviously used to at least some physical work. Yet his face was intelligent, handsome in a block featured sort of way. His chest was deep, the black hair matted thickly above his open shirt collar. On the stool to his right lay his jacket and tie. The woman was to his left.

"I don't come often," the woman answered awkwardly. She felt a faint, delicious but frightening stirring in her abdomen, a tightening in her chest.

The man looked at her left hand and saw there was no ring. He also observed the white line on her wedding finger, where one had recently been.

The woman noticed that the man was looking at her hand and glanced away across the bar. He knows I'm divorced, she thought. Or at least he knows I don't want to be taken for married. He understands why I'm here. She felt a sudden urge to get up and leave, to save at least something of her diminishing self-respect. But she did not.

"My name's Jack," the man said good-naturedly. "Jack Harnett. Sales and pump installation. But not oil wells unfortunately." He grinned cheerfully, looking at the woman with a visibly increased interest, sipping the refilled beer glass the bartender had brought. On the other end of the darkened lounge was a small fountain with colored lights mounted behind it. The different colors of the rotating lights reflected on his left cheek.

"I—I'm Janet," the woman said. She forced herself to go on. "Uh—what type of beer is that you're drinking?"

"Miller. Plain old Miller Draft," the man said, laughing and turning the glass in his big hand, as if searching for sediment in a vintage wine. He looked at her half empty glass.

"Scotch and soda," she said. She picked it up, lifting it gracefully, self-consciously to her lips.

The man smiled approvingly. Her breasts were smooth and creamy inside the black neckline of her dress.

In this way a conversation began, the conversation covering various general and unimportant topics, and gradually growing pleasant, friendly and warm.

Janet was sure she really liked this man, and she grew less and less inhibited as she considered this fact. She even ended up telling him how she had become divorced, relating many of the sordid details concerning her husband's infidelities. She explained that she and her former husband had had no children. "It only lasted two years," she added darkly, "most of that not in the bedroom." She was getting drunk. The man could see that she was young. He was a bit older.

"He lost a lot," the man commented dryly, looking at her with piercing blue eyes. "He's a fool." He smiled warmly. Janet met his smile with one of her own, dropping her eyes.

The man put his large, rough, warm hand on her arm. Janet felt the warmth go down to her pelvis, and her heart began to beat strongly. I don't care, she thought. What else can I do anyway?

"Let's get out of here," the man suggested.

Janet automatically picked up her purse. Her heart was beating very fast, though her head was swimming from the several strong drinks she'd had.

Janet and the man she'd met just an hour before got up from their stools, put money on the varnished, mahogany bar, and went outside into the night air.

Firebase Forty-six

The soldiers of the gun crew didn't have a fire mission, and they'd already cleaned and maintenanced their weapon, a one seven five millimeter howitzer. Days like this were common. The afternoon heat was stifling, and there was nothing to do but wait for some word from the fire control center.

"Hey, GI, you give me cigarette?" A village boy of eight or nine stood just outside the roll of concertina wire that marked the northwest perimeter of the firebase. His hair was cut very short, and a scar beginning a half inch above one eyebrow ran visibly into it. He was wearing shorts and a faded brown, button-up shirt.

"You're too young to smoke," a soldier answered from a distance of about thirty feet. He got up from where he'd just sat down upon a 'C' rations case to open a can of pork and lima beans. "You want some of this?" He held up the can.

"Sure. I eat."

"No. You have your own food. Rice. Lots of rice." The soldier bent over and got something out of the small 'C' rations box he had pulled from the case and set beside him. It was a dark green can like the one that contained his pork and lima beans, but larger in circumference, not as deep, and already opened. Turning it over onto the palm of his left hand, he emptied its contents, which included several hard crackers and a chocolate bar of the same shape, wrapped in tin foil. "Here." Dropping the crackers back into the can and setting the can down, he walked over to the perimeter wire.

The village boy was standing near a sandbag bunker, the top of which was about four feet above the ground. An M-60 machine gun was mounted on it. The bunker was inside the wire, the boy outside. The sun was hot. No one was either in or on the bunker. Just outside the concertina wire were two sets of bipod marks and a wooden stake, indicating the recent presence of a claymore antipersonnel mine. It had been removed for the day.

The soldier handed the boy the 'C' rations candy bar. Then he sat down in the dry, yellow dust on the ground next to the wire, leaning his back against the bunker. The bunker provided a very small amount of shade, for the sun was high in the sky. But the sandbags were cool. He wiped the sweat off his face with the sleeve of his jungle fatigues, his shirt open in the front. Beads of sweat ran down his bony, hairless chest and across his stomach. Artillery shells, going from some other unit to some unknown destination in the hills, boomed in the distance. He could feel it in the ground beneath him. "Where'd you get that scar?" he asked the boy, leaning forward and pointing toward the boy's forehead above the left eye.

The boy's mouth was full of chocolate. "Bomb," he said. "Bomb fall in my village." He spoke with a full mouth, holding his hand in front of it to insure that none of its contents would fall out.

"No. No bomb," the soldier said, leaning back again and covering his eyes with the back of his hand to shield them from the sun. The sunlight, though the sun was behind him, made everything intense. Removing his hand after a moment, he looked closely at the boy. "Mortar, maybe," he said.

"Mortar, yes." The boy smiled. He was missing an incisor on both sides of his two front teeth. "Kill my sister."

"I'm sorry," the soldier said. There was salt in his mouth. Salty sweat burned the corners of his lips and his chin where he'd shaved clumsily with a metal mirror. He wondered how the boy could smile when speaking of an incident which had killed his sister. Yet the soldier couldn't help smiling himself. Like so many other eight or nine year old boys, this one looked like a rodent with his two big front teeth and gaping holes on either side of them.

"Why do you want cigarettes?"

"Smoke." The boy moved two fingers toward and away from his lips, as if already smoking. "Give me smoke."

"No. It'll ruin your health." Then the soldier thought how ridiculous this statement was. Chances were the boy wouldn't live long enough to worry about his health. "Anyway, I don't smoke," he continued.

The boy pointed to the 'C' rations case lying on the ground a short distance away. "You have cigarette in there," he said hopefully.

"Oh, all right. What's it to me anyway?" The soldier got up off the ground, went over and pulled a small packet of cigarettes out of the case. "Here." He threw it over the perimeter wire from where he was standing. The pack sailed through the air in an arc and landed several yards from the boy.

The boy went over and picked the small packet of four cigarettes up off the ground, waved and started off toward his village, barefoot on the dirt path which ran a ways alongside the perimeter wire before descending the hill.

"Crazy kid," the soldier said, waving back.

A river rolled along slow and muddy below. Most of the brush had been cleared from the hillside. But across the river the jungle stretched unbroken, silent and green toward the mountains.

The Light that Failed

"But what can we do?" Sharon asks. "He *is* my father." She is speaking to her husband in hushed tones. It is late at night and they are in the den, so as not to be heard by Sam Morison, who has already gone to bed. Sharon picks a book off one of the mahogany shelves lining the four walls of the room from floor to ceiling. The book has gold lettering on its spine and is bound in soft leather. She opens it and lets the odor of its pages fill her mind. This always seems to relax her. "I know he looks and acts strange," she continues, laying the book gently on the large, polished oak desk at which her husband is seated. Her fingers are long and thin, her fingernails immaculate but unpainted. The wood of the desk is of a lighter hue than that of the bookshelves.

"He is a source of embarrassment," her husband says, getting up irritably. He paces to the other end of the room but does not reach for a book, as his wife has just done.

"Hush, Paul! He'll hear you."

"I don't give a damn. You saw him at the Everetts' the other night. First he insults Tom's way of making a living . . ."

"Speculating in corn futures, honey. Dad sees that as driving up prices and gambling on other people's fortunes and hard work."

"Well, maybe he's right. I don't think much of it myself. But you still have to be polite when you're a guest at someone else's home. Besides, Millie Everett is your friend, not mine. Weren't you embarrassed?"

"Yes. But Millie understands. She's met Dad before."

"Well, Tom certainly didn't look pleased. I wonder that he didn't pick the old rascal up and throw him out his front door."

"That wouldn't have been easy," Sharon says smiling. She has a thin upper lip and chiseled features, which give her a kind of fragile, china doll appearance. Paul looks at his wife, at the diamond earrings set like stars in the lobes of her small ears. She never takes them off until she goes to bed, he thinks absently. He wonders how the "warty" old man, with bushy, simian eyebrows and tufts of hair in his ears, could have spawned such a lovely creature. Even well into middle age, her small, shapely breasts protrude firmly through the thin silk of her housecoat. Now seated in the chair at the desk where he'd been seated a moment before himself, she crosses her legs, exposing slender, shapely calves, knees and thighs as the folds of the housecoat slip away. Her legs are, even after all these years, exquisite!

"What about his appearance?" Paul continues. "He's . . . he's some kind of anachronism. What with the long white beard, bent over walk, and stupid somber expression he always seems to . . ."

"He's not stupid."

"I know that. That's not what I said. Okay. The great professor of economics. Emeritus now. Whatever. The point is, he was always going to write the great book and never did. Going to prove that rents, profits and—what is it?—interest, yes. That they're all the same thing. How does he put it? Oh, yes." Paul lowers the pitch of his voice to make it sound pontifical. His wife's upper lip is drawn in with intense nervous irritation. She is afraid her father will awake and hear her husband. "'They are each of them themselves forms of speculation. Men gambling on an uncertain future of economic expansion. Today's inflated price, rent, service charge (call it interest, if you will)—today's margin of profit will be tomorrow's increased value. But that never happens. Progress is never the equal of speculative greed. So there is inflation, over-extension of credit, suppression of wages, or finally a market contraction, a recession or depression.' What does he say? 'Price must reassert its role in reflecting true value, real cost under the contending influences of labor, scarcity and . . . and sentiment!' Sentiment. Ha! What the hell is sentiment?"

"Paul, please. Calm down. At least, lower your voice. Dad will hear."

"I don't care what he hears!" Paul shouts at the top of his lungs. "The man's a crackpot," he adds in a lower tone. "Will you please cover your legs? I can't think."

"Well, excuse me!"

"Sharon. Listen. I know I sound like a jerk." Paul comes over to the chair and leans over, gently touching his wife's hair. "It was just so embarrassing last night. The man picks up one of Millie's china tea cups and says, 'This delicate, eggshell thin object of ostentation for the rich . . . ' He holds the damn thing up to the light, mind you: 'through which I see a false light, the light of modern industrial deceit.' My god, Sharon, who does this guy think he is? Oh, with the long beard and the white hair down to his collar. Uncombed. I'll tell you who he is. Moses. No, Elijah, by god. Hell, John the Baptist too. Maybe all of them together."

"Paul, sit down!" Sharon has gotten up from the chair and pushes her two hundred pound, six foot one husband into it. "I've heard enough, okay. I know he has embarrassed us. And no doubt he'll do it again. But there's nothing we can do about it. We aren't going to turn him out into the street. And maybe, just maybe he's right. He was a good teacher."

"At a small college."

"His colleagues respected him."

"He published little and certainly not the great book."

"He did his best."

"And failed."

"Yes," Sharon answers in a subdued tone, pushing her hair out of her face. "And failed. Maybe we're all failures, Paul. We all end up in the same place."

And what's taking *him* so long? Paul thought. But he didn't further express what he knew to be a cruel and unjust emotion.

A Tragic Death

Mildred Sipes was a woman of less than ordinary capability, it was said. This in spite of her education, her lifelong habit of study and reflective thought. It was because, as Mildred was a former schoolteacher now retired for many years, her neighbors had forgotten her profession. To them she was simply a strange old woman, poorly dressed due to a limited income, who lived in a small, shabby house. She talked to herself sometimes. Her once blond, now thinned white hair, hung like a rag to her shoulders. Her shoulders were stooped, rounded inward, as though to conceal or protect an introverted soul, like her curious habit of reading which few people ever witnessed.

Her house stood alone in a rain drenched meadow outside the little town of Monroe, Washington, at the foot of the Cascade Mountains, which seemed close enough to topple over onto it. There it was and nothing more: a wooden house covered with fading white paint; a mud enhanced, sparsely graveled drive; and rain and snow drenched evergreen forest all around. In short, Millie, as a few reliable acquaintances called her, was considered something of an anomaly, outside the general sphere of social events.

The postman was one of these acquaintances. He was a man in his thirties with a wife and five kids. If Millie came to the door when he delivered the mail, he always had a kind word for her. She, in turn, had once, in the previous year, invited him in on a cold morning a few days before Christmas for a quick cup of hot chocolate, and he had seen the books. They were everywhere: on the walls, scattered over the coffee table, stacked on the divider between the dining area and the kitchen, even on the floor. Though not a reader himself, this had impressed him. Millie was an intellectual, he decided. And this was not a thing to be trifled with.

Another even more recent acquaintance was the deputy sheriff who had pulled up and banged vigorously on her door one evening when he had seen smoke coming from her roof near the chimney. Millie was asleep in a recliner chair in her living room with a book open on her chest. The commotion at the door startled her. She ran to answer it. The volunteer fire department soon put out the small blaze. The damage was minimal. At any rate, such events were not uncommon for home owners who had cedar shake roofs.

Anthony, this deputy sheriff, dropped by occasionally after that to see how Millie was doing. He was one of those who were of the opinion that Millie was below water in matters of general alertness. But his view of her was, for the most part, benevolent.

Now Millie had a dog, a terrier of sorts. Its genealogy was very much in question. Nevertheless, it had certain very terrier-like traits: It was less than medium height, slender of build, brown and white, its hair coarse, curly and matted, as on a wire-haired fox terrier. It also had a bristly snout and bright, dark brown little eyes. Something like a smile seemed to play always about its face. It was mischievous, ornery, wayward, inordinately curious, and Millie loved it. The dog's name was Thornton. Such a name was itself one of the mysteries surrounding the character of Millie.

"Thornton. Thornton, you get home!" Millie called after dark one evening at her front door. Beside her, inside the entryway on the floor, was a dish of warm food. "Wherever could that little rascal be?" Millie wondered aloud, shaking her head. The moon was full in early December, and there was snow on the ground.

The snow, unusually heavy for the West Coast this winter, had fallen the previous morning, melted down a bit in the sunny afternoon, and become crusty in the cold that night. For this reason, the dog's tracks in it were clearly delineated. They went about mostly zigzag and in circles. But there was a line of them that went out beyond one side of the house toward a bush and stopped. That was where Thornton generally did his business. Millie thought she could detect in the clear moonlight another line that went pretty much straight ahead toward the woods across the thinly graveled driveway.

"Wherever you are, Mr. Thornton . . ." Millie sang out wistfully and shut the door without finishing her sentence. She shook her head again, smiling, somewhat stooped as always in her posture, as she reentered the warm interior of the house. The fireplace was blazing nicely, popping softly now and then. There was plenty of cordwood outside. She'd bought it from a local woodsman and paid a neighbor boy, who came around once in a while looking for work, a couple dollars to stack it. The woodsman had merely dumped it out of his pickup truck onto the ground.

Millie was at her books in the living room when the dog came home. At her feet were scattered tomes of Archimedes, Apollonius and Nicomachus. In her hands was a volume of the nineteenth century German mathematician, Karl Friedrich Gauss. For Millie had been a high school mathematics teacher and was interested in such arcane subjects as conic sections, the theory of numbers and probability distribution.

Millie heard Thornton's whining. She went and opened the door. Thornton marched in with a glove in his mouth. It was approximately ten o'clock at night.

* * *

The glove was in fairly good condition. It didn't look as if it had come out of someone's trash, or, as was more likely in these deserted parts, been tossed out the window of a pickup truck and then found alongside the road by Thornton.

Millie took the glove from the dog, affectionately ruffling his fur, and set the dish of now cold food before him. Thornton ate greedily, swallowing his food in mouth-sized chunks. His belly could be seen to swell into the shape of a barrel as he ate, every muscle in his legs and neck tensed and thrown into the execution of this task.

"Hungry are you?" Millie asked her pet. "Well, that'll put some warmth back into you." She examined the glove. Where could this have come from? she wondered.

By morning Mildred Sipes had hatched an idea. When she sent Thornton out to do his morning business, she would keep an eye on him. This she did.

Sure enough, it was just as she suspected, or at least hoped. Having deposited his load, the dog headed straight for the woods in the direction he had gone the previous morning. There was still snow on the ground, though it had melted away in places, leaving patches of mud. Being careful to avoid these, Millie set out after her dog. His tracks were plainly visible.

Ten minutes into the woods, she came upon Thornton. He was sniffing gingerly at something in the snow, repeatedly jerking his nose back. There was a dark, slender object sticking up from the ground. It looked like an arm and gloved hand.

Millie's stomach tightened. She glanced about as if she expected to find a dangerous intruder. "Thornton," she called, immediately recognizing the feebleness of her voice. "Thornton!" she repeated firmly. The dog looked back at her.

"Come away from there."

The dog stretched his neck out, the snout on the end of it like a sensitive finger, and took one more sniff. Then he ran up to Millie, wagging his tail.

Millie went immediately home without further investigation. But within a few minutes she left the house again to return to the mysterious sight. She stopped at the edge of the same clearing she had been in when she had come upon her dog. This time she had left him locked up in the house. That was rather foolish, she thought. He has better senses than I do.

Since Millie was standing at a point several yards distant from the point she'd been standing at before, she saw things from a different perspective. The body—it was clearly the body of a young man—was lying on its back, one arm extended frozen into the air. The other arm was on the ground, missing a glove.

At home again, Millie sat for some time in her living room, surrounded by her books. It was the most reassuring place she could think of to be while clearing her mind. Her muscles felt as if they were enmeshed in a cobweb of steel. She couldn't move. The room was dark. It was cold. The fire was out. Both the front and back door were locked.

It would be hard to say how long Millie might have remained in that position, if she had not heard the postman outside. She heard the vehicle, then the squeak of her mailbox. It was a series of sounds that entered the long, cold, dark tunnel of her house and traveled to her ear. The sounds penetrated her, glowing with warmth as she recognized their probable source. Millie arose suddenly and dashed through the front door.

She must've looked like a mad woman, her white hair flying as she descended the three wooden steps that led up to her door, her heavy coat concealing all but the frilly hem of a nightgown, her bare white legs blotched blue by the marks of varicose veins. The postman stepped back in dismay, a look of alarm in his eyes. He dropped a letter on the ground beside the steps.

"Oh, Fred! Freddie, you've got to help me!" Millie exclaimed.

"Wha . . . what's the matter?" He retrieved the letter from the ground in an effort of calming himself.

Millie was at his side now, gesticulating toward the woods. There was an overcast gray sky, probably promising more snow. The air had picked up an added feeling of coldness and damp. "I think there's a dead man out there. No, a young fellow. I know he's dead." These words burst forth from her, but their release steadied her nerves. Never had she been so happy to be in the presence of human company before. Not that she liked being alone. The myth of her reclusiveness was an unkind invention of her neighbors. Neighbors she rarely saw anyway.

The young postman accompanied Millie into the woods. He had never seen a dead person before. Of course, neither had Millie. The dead person was simply dead. His eyes were open. But they were not like the eyes of the living. They were like an empty book, Millie reflected. As if nothing had ever been written in them. The postman did not make an observation to himself. He was a simple man.

They observed that the victim was very young, between eighteen and twenty perhaps. Neither of them recognized him. They did not disturb the body but returned to the house and called the sheriff. Then the postman left, for he had a route to finish.

Millie, now a good deal calmer, cooked herself up a mess of scrambled eggs. She did this on an old wood stove. The phone, lights and decent plumbing were her only modern conveniences.

She dumped the eggs on a plate, sniffed them, and scraped the contents of the plate into the dog's dish. Then she sat down to wait for the deputy sheriff. Outside the kitchen window, a light, chilly snow was beginning to fall from a darkened sky.

* * *

Anthony was the deputy sheriff who came to Millie's door. He happened to be on duty and had picked up the call on his radio. The dispatcher readily turned the matter over to him.

Anthony had someone with him when Millie opened her front door. He was a young man, a volunteer who was part of the sheriff's auxiliary. Anthony, Millie and the young man—who had been introduced to her as Bob—went into the woods. The body was there, a powdering of snow on its face, gloved hand and extended arm. The ice crystals in the eyelashes of the dead man gave him the look of one who had come from far away through great hardship. Millie shuddered in her nightgown and overcoat, for she still hadn't gotten properly dressed. The deputy sheriff looked over at her but said nothing.

"Appears to be dead, all right," the young man observed with gravity. He was standing directly over the corpse but did not venture further. The deputy sheriff thought he detected a shudder in this young man as well.

"Bob," he said, "why don't you head on back to the car and get County up on the radio. See if dispatch can get someone out here from the morgue."

After Bob had gone, Anthony went over to the body. Millie kept her distance and watched. She wished she had eaten something. She was feeling a bit queasy. The deputy sheriff pulled on the arm, but the body appeared to be frozen to the ground. The glove came off and exposed a startling white hand, whiter somehow, it seemed, than the other one on the ground. Snow was now falling heavily, and the air was like ice, stinging both the deputy's and Millie's cheeks and ears.

"Frozen solid," the deputy said.

Millie made a mental note of the fact and determined to remain indoors for the rest of the day.

Anthony leaned over, pulling the knit, dark blue wool cap from the young man's head. There were no abrasions or lacerations. No sign of foul play anywhere on the body, insofar as he could see. Hypothermia, he decided, though the man was well clothed for harsh weather. "Must've lost his way," he said aloud.

"Who?"

"Must've lost his way," the detective repeated.

"Oh," Millie said.

The detective pulled a pack of matches out of a front pocket of the young man's trousers. They were dry and in good condition. "Damn!" he said and put the matches back into the pocket. He offered no further comment.

Back at the house, the ambulance arrived and then left with the body. The frozen corpse had been loaded into the cold white bowels of the thing right next to Millie's old Buick, and she had shuddered once again involuntarily, reflecting that the Buick had been asleep for nearly a week and nothing, fortunately, could awaken it short of the ignition key. There was much irrelevant radio chatter to be heard from one of the two vehicles left in the yard, and Anthony spent a long time in it writing up the preliminaries of a report. Bob took it upon himself to comfort the "old woman."

"Must've lost his way," he said, repeating what the deputy had told him. Bob and Millie were standing just inside the front door of the house, where they had been observing events unfolding in the yard. "Got too far out and didn't know where he was in the snow storm a couple days ago," he went on. "Poor fellow. Just imagine. He was only a short distance from your house. Could've saved himself if he'd known it."

When Bob observed that his comforting words were not having their desired effect—the look in Millie's eyes was one of horror and guilt—he added by way of amendment, "Chances are, he was already out of his head with the hypothermia. Probably didn't know where he was at all. No way for you to know about it either."

Anthony arrived in time to avert a breakdown on the part of one or the other. "There's something I haven't asked you, Millie," he said, stepping inside the door. This deputy had dark eyes, almost black, which were hard as beads and gentle like chocolate at the same time. He also had a sallow, sunken-cheeked, pockmarked face. He was obviously a smoker, must've worn dentures, had some rough teen years, and probably tipped a bottle now and then during his off hours. All of these were unconscious observations which Millie had made in the past without thinking about it. "What led you to go into the woods on such a day in the first place?"

"It was Thornton, who brought home a glove last night. I followed him out there this morning."

"Thornton?" Anthony thought, then remembered the little dog, which was nowhere to be seen due to its fear of strangers. "Ah, I see," he said. "Well, listen, Ms. Sipes, I've got to be going in to make out my report, but I can drop back by a little later, if you like,"

"I'll be all right," Millie said.

Bob was beaming with youthful good will. Anthony was accomplishing what he, Bob, had intended.

"Okay," the deputy said. "Don't worry. We'll take it from here." He wondered if Millie had understood the events she had helped to unfold. "It's good you called us," he added. Then he turned and left with his young partner.

After heating a tubful of water in the charcoal-fueled water heater which was housed in a small shed attached to the outside of the house, Millie gave herself a good soaking. She knew Anthony estimated her intelligence at far below its true value, but this didn't bother her. What she was concerned with was how the frozen young man in the woods—now in the cold white, rolling freezer chest, and who had appeared in the woods quite suddenly like Sasquatch, the legendary Bigfoot monster of Washington State—well, how had he gotten to where he was in the first place? There wasn't another house in sight. Why was he there? And what was it like to die so alone?

* * *

The deputy did not drop by the house again later in the afternoon. That was what he understood Millie to want. She needed to work it out alone.

This she did, or tried to do. Millie had an old Buick, which, as mentioned before, had just been given a good week's nap. But it was also in need of repair. It was a dependable car overall. That is to say, the engine ran well. But the heater didn't work.

After her bath and the preparation of a second breakfast, which she consumed, Millie decided to drive into town. She did not express the matter to herself in certain terms, but she instinctively felt the need to be around living people.

"Now don't you go finding any more surprises," she said to her dog as she released him into the yard. He ran straight off to the woods to find what was no longer there.

Millie got into her car and went into town, where she bought a few groceries. After that, there wasn't much to do, so she headed toward home. She hadn't said anything to anybody about the incident. She wasn't sure she wanted to talk about it, and no one had so much as said hello to her anyway. It wasn't that they were unfriendly. They were going about their own business and had not recognized her presence as an unusual event. It wasn't.

The snow had never completely stopped falling that day. It came and went in flurries, usually pushed along by an icy gust of wind. This wind was coming off Puget Sound, not through the Snoqualmie mountain pass where Interstate 90 ran. The wetness of it made that evident.

"Brrr!" Millie had remarked after loading her groceries into the trunk of her car. It was during one of those high-velocity snow flurries. The sky was close and dark.

Millie drove slowly. She always did. Impatient young bucks in pickup trucks were forever passing her on the road. They were the ones who blasted holes in all the rural stop signs, she was sure. Not that she'd ever seen one of them do it. But most of them had a rifle or shotgun or two hanging from hooks in the rear of the cab of their trucks. The guns could be seen through the rear window. Besides, upon closer inspection once or twice, she had detected a low forehead and close-set eyes.

Instead of turning off toward home, Millie did an irresponsible thing. Irresponsible because the heater wasn't working in her car.

She headed for Seattle. It was only an hour away, and the bright show windows on the stores around Fourth and Pine might cheer her up. It wasn't that she was depressed. She just wasn't ready yet to share her neck of the woods with the ghost of the young man.

Millie spent several hours in the Bon Marche, a department store in a multistoried white building which had beautiful show windows on the first floor. There was also a huge star made of white lights that extended in a cheerful ray down one side of the building. It was several weeks before Christmas, and the interior of the store was jammed with people, especially on the main floor displaying perfume and jewelry. Even up on the floor where furniture was sold there were quite a few customers. People like her, milling around soaking in the excitement and vitality of the busy atmosphere.

Millie found something in the bargain basement to lift her spirits: an exotic looking pair of slippers of a Moroccan design. She also picked up a novel in the book section. It was a Trollope she hadn't read: *The Eustace Diamonds*. She found Trollope's genteel style soothing. Life could be troublesome without being a complete disaster. That was reassuring. This was not a time for *King Lear*.

On the way home Millie remarked to herself on the cold. Her gloved hands could feel the iciness of the steering wheel. Outside her windshield the black road glittered with snow crystals that kept falling and melting. It wasn't that they were melting because the air was warm. Darkness had already fallen, and it certainly wasn't. But the pavement must've retained a little heat. Though heat from what, Millie didn't know. She hadn't seen the sun all day.

The snow drifted past her windshield and was pounded into water by her wipers. But it accumulated on her side and rear windows. She kept rolling the driver's side window down to remove the snow. It blew in and stung her face.

Finally, when a diesel rig blared its horn and passed her in a blaze of indistinguishable light, she knew she had to stop. The big truck had frightened her, and she needed to clear the snow off the back window so she'd see the next one coming.

Out in the wet snow and wind, Millie held her coat tightly to her body with one arm while she brushed away the cold, white, crinkly powder with the other. It was several inches thick and made her hand ache. She looked about, but no cars were coming.

She got back into the car. It started easily as always. But when she attempted to steer off the gravel shoulder onto the pavement, she spun out somehow on some snow and black ice and one rear wheel slid off the outside of the shoulder, which dropped several feet toward the woods. The car was now resting on one side of its frame. She couldn't move it. She could only spin the rear wheels.

Though her heart was beating rapidly, Millie calmly shut off the engine and headlights. She'd heard you should leave the hood up if you wanted help, so she got out and did that. Getting back into the car, she turned on the flashers.

Where are all the cars now? she wondered. The road was inky dark and deserted. Forest rose up on either side. You could almost hear the snow falling. She thought of the young man.

* * *

The young man had lain in the snow impervious to the cold. It must've been different earlier on. She was glad she wasn't there to see it then. Of course, she could've helped him if she had been. But she had to admit to herself that she was glad she hadn't known about it until it was over. Millie shivered. She realized she could well be headed toward the same fate now.

In spite of all the windows being rolled up tight, the car was getting cold. She could feel the cold down near the foot pedals, creeping up her legs. It was like the description of Socrates she had read in one of Plato's dialogues. After he had drunk the poison hemlock, which the Athenian government had so generously provided free of charge—governments were always helpful that way—the coldness of death had made its way from his extremities toward his heart. His feet and legs had felt cold first. Was she already shutting down? No!

She was amazed at how little terror she felt overall. She was scared to death, but it was a calm fear. She trusted God. Do you hear that, Lord? I'm trusting in you to get me out of this. Please. Well, it was in his hands.

Why should she, a woman in her sixties, have a greater right to life than a young man? She didn't know. Why was his right arm sticking up in the air like that? How did it get that way? What was he doing when he died? What does one do anyway in such a death, all alone in the dark?

Why were there suddenly no cars on the road? Was God testing her? With a sinking heart she reasoned that she knew better. There were no cars because the weather and roads were so nasty. She was on her own, and morning was a long way off. It was as simple as that. An eternity. She was sitting in a void where there was no time, just as there was no light. She could hear the snow falling. That was all. And feel its numbing encroachment.

Yes. The coldness inside the car was crushing in on her like a vise now. It had hands of steel. The car was made out of steel. Life itself was as indifferent and uncaring as cold steel. Millie felt the hot tears on her cheeks. She held her heavy coat tight against her chest. It seemed to have no power to hold out the cold. Millie had always preferred mathematics to mysteries. But she had also retained something of a belief in some sort of transcendent being who watched over her fate. She prayed fervently to him now. Please, Lord . . . We have all had such moments.

Exhausted from prayer, Millie began to feel sleepy. She wasn't quite as cold. She shook herself. She knew what that meant.

The windshield and all the other windows of the car were covered with snow. It was like being sealed in her tomb. No! Well, what did it matter? She observed with satisfaction that the indicator lights for the flashers were still going. Maybe . . . She could hope.

What a strange coincidence that she should share the same fate as the young man and practically on the same day. There was less than forty-eight hours difference. Certainly not more. God had a sense of humor. And a perverse one! If there was a God. Forgive me, Lord. I'm frightened. Please, please help me.

Millie sat inside her iron tomb. She did not feel quite as frightened now, since the cold seemed to have abated. She was in a kind of wistful, dreamy state, and this left her free to exercise, in some measure, her favorite pursuit: abstract contemplation.

What is death anyway? What is life? Bodies decay, but is that just a change on the apparent surface of reality? Who do those folks think they are who insist there is a substantial difference? How could they know? They're only on one side of the revolving door and can't see what's on the other.

Millie came out of her reverie with a start. It was as if a blade had pierced her heart. When she sat up, it felt as if she were swimming in heavy water. She felt unbearably hot, and panic seized her. This was a panic without any name: a pure, undiluted pounding of the heart and pulsing at the temples. Pure because it had no apparent cause in the character of her thoughts.

Millie threw open the door on the driver's side of the car. She climbed out and trudged several feet into the snow, the fresh portion of which on the side of the road was eight inches deep. The snow had stopped falling. There was no wind. And the moon had broken through the clouds. The tall, pointed evergreens along either side of the road were clearly delineated. The tops of the hemlocks among them leaned over in sad, weary stillness.

Millie was burning as with a fever. She unbuttoned her coat and threw it on the ground—there in the snow beside the car. Then she trudged off heavily into the woods. Her legs and feet were like wooden posts. They had no feeling and seemed to jar into her conscious abdomen with every step. Her gait was clumsy, but she pressed forward and went in deep among the trees. Then somewhere among their dark trunks, in a clearing lit up with moonlight as though with a halo, she saw the young man. He was standing calmly. The look on his face was warm and gentle. He held up his right hand as if to stay her, an expression of kindness in his eyes. Millie had been in the process of unbuttoning her blouse. She fell unconscious into the snow.

* * *

It is not decided whether Millie should've died that night. When found by a passing trucker—who noticed her flashers, the open door of the car, lit interior, coat discarded in the snow, footprints leading off into the forest—her vital signs were few: her flesh cold, her pulse and breathing difficult to determine. But whatever remained of life, congealed in the chilled center of her being, was kept alive at Harborview Medical Center in Seattle. Fortunately, she hadn't driven very far from the city before her car had gotten stuck.

At home, perhaps a week later, when the mailman was making his usual round, he remarked how happy he was that she had come through, for he had heard of her ordeal from Anthony, the deputy sheriff.

"I'm fine now," Millie said, standing at her door, ignoring the fact that she had suffered severe frostbite in her feet and had had several toes removed. Her feet were still bandaged from the operation.

Fred had brought her mail up to her just for the occasion of making his comment.

"God sent the young man to me," Millie said.

The postman looked at her quizzically.

"Out there in the woods," she continued. "When I saw him, I was sure I'd be all right." She smiled.

The postman left. Perhaps Anthony was right, he decided, driving on down the road. The old woman was a little under the water in judgment. But if a hallucination comforted her, what was it to him?

Sometime after that Millie went quietly into the woods with her dog one morning and set up a small, wooden cross where the young man's body had been found. Then she made a point of never returning to the spot.

Small Corner of the World

Ann Morgan sat on a tall, wooden bar stool in the Old Tin Star and took a mouthful of beer, savoring it, rolling it around on her tongue and swishing it into her cheeks before she swallowed it. The beer glass was cold, tapered narrow at the bottom, and she found herself unconsciously drawing lines in the condensed vapor on its outer surface. She was dressed in blue jeans and a man's blue flannel shirt, which hung loosely outside her jeans. The shirt was too big and the indigo blue color of it contrasted sharply with her carrot red hair, which she kept pinned back in a tight bun. She was a large but thin, raw-boned woman, densely freckled with a narrow, slightly hooked nose. She might have been called handsome but never pretty.

"I don't see why you have to be that way," said the man sitting next to her. He got off his bar stool and laid some money next to his empty beer glass. The bartender came over and the man said, "Keep the change." Then, turning back to Ann, he continued, "It only happened once. It would never happen again." His tone was pleading.

"I know that, John," Ann said. "But feelings aren't the same now. I will always think of you as a good friend."

"I don't want to be your friend. That's not the way it was." The man turned angrily and walked out of the room. He went into the adjacent steak house, passing through an archway into a hall and then through a small door into the restaurant.

Ann sat for some time, both hands cupped about her beer glass. She was slowly nursing it, not wanting to drink enough to lose control. "Damn it all!" she muttered to herself.

"You need something, Ann?" The bartender came over. He was a heavy, jolly looking man, his high blood pressure giving him a ruddy, grainy, almost purplish complexion. He laid his fat hand on the counter. The knuckles were large, white and hairy. "I wouldn't let him get to you," he said, leaning over and pointing a finger at her with a friendly smile.

"Sure," Ann said. "You haven't seen Mark Shorfeld, have you? He hasn't been in today?"

"No. But he was in a short time last night. Some kind of anthrax problem with his cattle."

"Anthrax!"

"Well, that's what he was saying. But you know Mark. Doesn't know cows anyway."

"Yeah sure." Ann chuckled. She had a deep voice for a woman.

"If it was to rain some now, Mark'd be out there building an ark."

Ann laughed. "Sure could use some of that rain," she said.

"That's for sure." The bartender went off to attend to another customer.

Ann drifted back into her own thoughts. This was her third glass, and the beer was working on her. She felt a little hazy and melancholy. Until two years ago when her husband, Sam Morgan, had died suddenly and unexpectedly of a heart attack, she had been a happy woman. Their small ranching operation, a few miles west of the town of Emmett, Idaho, and not far from the east Oregon state line, had paid enough to keep them in necessities, not to mention a few pleasantries, and they had had no children anyway.

"Hello Ann," a quiet, somewhat refined voice said. The man spoke in an eastern accent.

She turned to find Mark Shorfeld on the stool to her left. "Hello," she answered in a husky tone. "How's the anthrax?" She kept a neutral expression on her face.

"Dan's been telling you stories."

"Not me!" The bartender grinned, figuratively putting him off with a big hairy right arm, hand extended upward, five fingers spread.

"Well." Ann cleared her voice. She seemed to have trouble talking to Mark. He was a handsome man, and he was single, operating the small ranch next to hers. "I've been meaning to tell you. BLM's planning to close off some of its pasture this summer in the Payette River Valley. We're going to have a tough time finding enough forage for our cattle this year."

"Doesn't matter. I'm cutting out."

"What!"

"Going back east. I've put the place up for sale."

Ann stared at Mark, unable to speak. She turned to her beer and took a drink, washing her mouth with it before swallowing it. The beer was getting warm. The taste of hops seemed stronger. It made her think of the endless gridlike pattern of hop fields with their tall wooden supports for the hop vines. The huge dinosaurlike wood structures appeared like ghosts all over the flat barren plains in the early morning spring fog of Southwestern Idaho south and west of the mill and farming town of Emmett. Her head really seemed to swim now, but she wasn't sure it was the beer. An acrid, almost metallic odor of beer and spirits filled the dark, stuffy room. There were various voices. Billiard balls clanked in a corner of the room. The outside door opened and a beam of light flooded the bar then was cut off into darkness again as the door swung shut. Several new figures stood just inside the door, but their features were indistinguishable due to the sudden contrast of light and dark and its effect on Ann's eyes. "I can't believe it," Ann said quietly, turning back around after looking at the door, holding her beer glass in both hands and looking straight ahead over the bar counter, her elbows propped on top of it. "I just can't believe it."

"I'm sorry, Ann," Mark said, pressing her wrist warmly. "I'm just not a rancher. Never was. You know that." He drank off his single beer and left. Mark's property adjoined hers on the east and northeast.

Ann had a number of beers after that. She didn't care. What did it matter? What did anything matter? Life was so empty. She was careful not to think of Sam. He wouldn't approve of her weakness. But then what business was it of his, going off and leaving her alone the way he did?

Ann was at the Old Tin Star until late. The friendly bartender went off duty and another came on shift. She didn't know him, so she kept to her own thoughts. No one bothered her. She was one of the last customers to leave the lounge.

Sheep's Wool

Sheep do not excel in intellectual matters. They have large and sensitive eyes, expressing a sort of indiscriminate wonder and kindness. It is an innocent kindness which causes even the gentlest man to feel the wolf within him. Perhaps in most of us there is at least something of the predator. In the sheep there is none. So innocent and giving is the nature of a typical sheep that, should a pair of shearing clippers, in passing over the warm, tight, round belly of such an animal, nick its taut flesh, the wound will unzip. It will open readily like a purse to reveal its innermost being.

This is the reason that most people do not like a sheep upon closer acquaintance. It makes them feel both vulnerable and cruel. Tom Watson was such a sheep, and most men eagerly despised him. Women, of a more forgiving demeanor, accepted his softness but felt sexually cold in his presence.

Tom lived his entire life alone in various Eastern cities. Like a good many people, he had few true friends but many acquaintances. He was short, undefined in his facial features, and shaped like a pear. He kept his hair close cropped. His fingers were stubby. All was simplicity in the habits and appearance of this man. All but one thing: almost everywhere he went he carried a camera and frequently a bag full of auxiliary equipment, such as lenses, filters and different grades of film.

Now, if the person of this man was nondescript in the eyes of the world, his work was not. Many recognized the clear simple truth that showed through his pictures. In a fraction of a second, in the click of a shutter, he could freeze-dry a human story of pathos and longing.

For this, at the age of forty-five, Tom was rewarded with an exhibition of his work at the Museum of Modern Art in New York City. Though a resident of Philadelphia for more than a decade, he was present for the occasion. The majority of these photographs had been published at one time or another in various magazines. But they had never before been seen together. Many of them black and white, all of them strung out in a horizontal line on bare white walls, like a moving picture, they were extraordinary!

"This one," a young woman said, passing through the exhibit on a wintry afternoon. It was a good place to get out of the cold. "It seems so simple yet cruel." She leaned her blond head on the shoulder of a man in his early twenties.

Her companion bent forward to get a closer look. "They're playing some sort of stick ball in an alley," he said. "They look happy enough."

The young lady moved a slender wrist toward a small plaque which gave the title of the photograph. "Boys in North Philadelphia," she read. She frowned, looking at the photograph.

The young man was now interested in a single detail which he examined with careful attention. "Ugh." He stepped back suddenly. The young lady, who was attached, or clinging, to his right arm, was startled by the abrupt movement, which set her ungracefully off balance. "What's the matter?" she asked.

"Well, take a look here."

"Where? The shadow?" The woman leaned forward. "Oh!" She straightened suddenly. "It's a dog!"

"Yes. Very dead. Decomposing, I would say, in the middle of the street."

"How horrible!"

"They're using it for a base."

"Oh, Jon, let's leave."

"Ha ha ha." The man started to laugh. "What an ingenious idea!"

"Oh, Jon, don't be disgusting. Couldn't they have found something better for the purpose? I mean, really, a rotting corpse for a base!"

"Got to use what's available, I guess. There are plenty of starving wild dogs in Philadelphia, I've heard. The City of Wild Dogs."

"That's Baltimore."

"I know that, Nora." Jon was proud of what he knew, especially in the presence of his woman, who should not pretend to know as much. They moved down to another photograph.

"Who's that funny little guy over there watching us?" Nora whispered in her boyfriend's ear.

The boyfriend turned around. The man, across the room and shaped like a pear, was carrying a camera bag. There was a thirty-five millimeter camera slung about his neck. He tried to be casual but was clearly observing them. Such was his physical appearance though, that the boyfriend felt no challenge. "I don't know," he said. "Some amateur who wants to imagine he's an important photographer, I guess. Looks like he might be a little sweet on you too." He snickered.

"Jon, you're so rude!" She glanced across the room. "Poor fellow." It was clear to her that he was an unfortunate sort of person.

Jon and Nora continued to enjoy the exhibit. There was a snapshot of a man who certainly looked disturbed. He was walking along next to an eight foot chain link fence, head bent over, pistol in one hand hung at his side, finger on the trigger. He appeared to be muttering. No one was near him. Who would have been so foolish as to be near him?

Then there was the woman in another picture. She was clearly distraught, a black woman of middle age. She too was bent over, practically resting on one knee, her fist shoved against the door of a row house, her legs heavy, her nylons ending at just below the knee. Her face was contorted in some sort of expression of grief or agony. She was apparently pounding desperately on that door. But what she was shouting between her tears, no one in the room could hear. Beside her, to the left, was the boarded up door of another row house apartment. To the right of this door was a broken window.

All of these pictures were labeled *North Philadelphia, Beyond Gerard Avenue*, or some other such epithet indicating the same general neighborhood in north-central Philadelphia. On other walls were different photographs, shot in other locales, but equally intense.

The Robbery

It was three o'clock in the morning at the all night convenience store. The lights were on inside the store and in the gas pump area under an adjacent but separate metal awning. They shone yellow against the outside darkness. At two a.m. Tom Morgan had slipped most of the cash from his register into a slot in the floor behind the checkout counter inside the store. He could not open the floor safe. The store manager, who would relieve him at seven, had the only key.

Outside, a car pulled up to the gas pumps. It looked as if it might be an old '58 Chevy Impala, partially restored, but still in need of a paint job. A rough looking man got out of the car and came into the store.

"Hey!" He swung the entrance door open. "How 'bout turning on the gas." The man was somewhere in his thirties, lean and muscular, with a full, scraggly, black beard. His hair was relatively short, uneven at the neck. He wore faded blue jeans and a white tee shirt. The tee shirt was dirty and, even at several yards distance from the counter to the door, Tom could see grease under the man's nails.

The customer stood angrily in the doorway. Tom looked at him.

"Did you hear me? I said turn on the gas."

"I can't do it until you pay."

"Here." The man threw a wadded up, grimy, five dollar bill on the counter and went out.

Tom turned the pump on. The man ran the gas until it went to well above twelve dollars. As he was filling his tank, a woman got out of the car and came into the store. Tom could see that there was someone else in the car, but he couldn't make the person out.

The woman wandered slowly toward the far end of the store, dawdling here and there along one of the long rows of shelves, past the packaged junk food, then small household items, to the beer and soda coolers on the wall. The coolers were on the opposite side of the store from the cash register and check-out counter. The counter was to the immediate left of the front door.

"You got any Dr. Pepper?" the woman asked loudly across the room. She was standing, holding a cooler door open, at the end of the long, double row of shelves she had passed.

"We're all out, ma'am."

"Ma'am?" The woman laughed a giggling sort of laugh. "I like that. Yes ma'am. No ma'am." The woman was wearing tight jeans showing the outline of her vaginal area. A light blue work shirt was tucked into them. She was slender and blond, attractive in a hard sort of way. Her voice was a smoker's voice, scratchy and hoarse.

"Whatsa matter, Tess?" The man with the beard had reentered the store.

"Nothin'," she said, popping some gum. "They ain't got no Dr. Pepper."

"Figures."

Tom stood stiffly behind the register. He thought he'd seen the woman pick something up off a shelf and slip it into her shirt on her way down the aisle. But he wasn't sure. He heard a car door slam and, looking through the plate glass front door of the store, saw a second man walk from the car toward him. This one was clean shaven but, if anything, he looked meaner than the first. He was very tall, wearing shower clogs and baggy khaki shorts and had big, bony knees and feet.

"Harley, what's takin' so long? You and Tess makin' sugar back there while I sit in the car?" As he entered the store, the first man was in the back, saying something in a low voice to Tess. The clerk couldn't hear it.

The second man walked over to the clerk. "What's your name?"

"Tom."

There was no traffic on the street, no one else at the gas pumps.

"Listen, Tom. You listen close." As he said this in a low, clear voice, he pulled a small black revolver out of his belt from under his shirt. Tom couldn't understand how he hadn't seen it. "You open the register and the safe. Now! And don't give me no shit."

"Yes sir."

"That's right. You do as I tell you."

With surprising swiftness, the two at the far end of the store had moved to the counter. The young woman grabbed several packs of cigarettes off the rack on the counter, stuffed them into her shirt, and went out the front door.

These guys are amateurs, Tom thought. But he wasn't sure what they would do. He popped the drawer of the cash register open and pulled the bills out of each slot: twenties, tens, fives and ones. There was little more than a hundred dollars there. He handed it to the clean-shaved man. The man kept the gun pointed at his face.

"Where's the rest of it?" the man said.

"That's . . ."

"The safe, fool! You want me to blow your brains out right now?" He was shouting. "I know you got a safe here."

"Yes, sir, but I can't get into it." Tom pulled back the little, brown, cloth rug, which was on the floor under his feet, and lifted a rectangular lid that matched the tile of the floor. Beneath it was a round safe hole four or five inches in diameter. The lid to this was closed, fitting perfectly in the hole, with a key slot in the center of it. Harley had gone around the counter to see. He appeared to be unarmed.

"Open the safe," Harley said.

"I can't. I don't have the key."

"You expect me to believe that?" The clean shaved man pressed the gun to Tom's temple. Tom felt the cold steel. His stomach was tight.

Harley had gotten down on one knee to look at the safe. He got up. "Let's get outa here," he said. He was close enough for Tom to smell his breath. It had a strange, acrid odor.

"This sonofabitch is lying," the man with the gun insisted.

A set of headlights flashed along the street as a single car went by.

"I said let's get out of here!"

The two men went out the door and got into the car. They drove away. Tom could not read the license plate. It was covered with dried mud.

Temporary Quarters

The rat was large, gray, obese. Looking down from a second story window of the Seattle Housing Authority apartment on Yesler Avenue, they could see it rummaging among the refuse of old bottles, cans and boards. There was no garbage lying about. Nevertheless, the rat was there. There on the bare ground now, sitting on its haunches, looking up at them with its beady black eyes. The couple watched it, leaning on the old, wooden window casement, staring at it with a peculiar fascination. The rat wriggled its nose, giving out a high pitched squeak. Its whiskers stood out like electric wires, alive, sensitive, reading the air.

"I think it wants us to give it some food," the man chuckled. "Go on, Rosie. Get some bread out of the fridge. Let's see what it does." The man was a little overweight himself, young with light blue eyes and a sandy colored butch haircut.

"Uh!" Rosie shuddered, pulling her bathrobe over her naked breasts and vigorously rubbing her shoulders. Across the empty expanse of ground in front of her, her husband and the open window, some thirty to forty yards away, was another wooden building similar to their own. In its aged appearance, it was essentially a long plywood box with so many windows. All of its windows were dark. Several were broken, which is a fact they had originally noticed in daylight. It was now ten o'clock at night.

"Go on, Rosie," the man said anxiously. "I want to see what it'll do."

Rosie went out of the room and downstairs to the kitchen. From that other distant room, or on the way back from it, she shouted,

"Why should we feed a filthy rat? We don't hardly have enough for ourselves, Ben."

"Shhh. Damn! You've gone and scared it away. Look what you've done."

Rosie had already reappeared beside her husband with a slice of bread. She glanced reluctantly out the window at the spot where she'd seen the rat before.

"Small loss," she said matter-of-factly.

"Give me a piece of that." Ben tore off a bit from the slice Rosie held in her hand. "See. Look. There it is." The rat had run under a board that was propped at one of its ends on an overturned, one gallon paint can. The board was still damp from the almost continuous drizzle of the Western Washington February weather. Presently the rat appeared atop the board, settling onto its haunches and peering up at them again. Though it was pitch black outside, with a cloud overhang and no moon, a downstairs light was on, and it was that light, shining through the downstairs living room window of the apartment, that illuminated the rat. There was no rain falling. But a chilling damp blew in through the window, a dampness of both weather and poverty, smelling of wet grass, moldy boards and the old, cracked, concrete, oil soaked pavement of the parking lot out in front of the building.

Ben dropped the piece of bread onto the bare, wet spot of ground where the rat had originally been. "Come on boy. There's your dinner. Go get it," he whispered hoarsely.

Rosie laughed, laid the remainder of the slice of bread down on the window sill and retreated into the center of the room. She sat down on a bed, the only piece of furniture in the room, and removed her robe. Ben looked over at his wife. She smiled back at him. She did not have a stitch of clothing on. She was an angular woman, darkly sexual.

"Be with you in a minute," Ben said, turning back to the open window. A damp gust of night air rustled past him. "Aren't you cold?"

"Nope." Rosie lay down on her back and pulled her legs up onto the bed, leaving them a little apart. The room had a musty smell, and she lay there and wondered how many people had been in that apartment before her and Ben. "Hundreds," she guessed aloud.

"Huh? What'd you say, Rosie?" Ben half turned from the window.

"Nothin'. I was just wonderin' how many folks'd been in this temporary housing before us."

"Plenty," Ben said. "More'n you can count, I reckon. There he goes!" Ben turned back into the window and leaned out to get a better look. The rat had, after a moment's hesitation, scuttled off the board and into the open space where the piece of bread was. The bread shone white in the downstairs light. The rat nibbled delicately, squeaking happily, then voraciously consumed the morsel. Ben picked up the remainder of the slice, squeezed it into a ball and dropped it out the window. It landed directly behind the rat. The rat started, then turned around and attacked the wad of bread.

"Are you coming, honey? I'm falling asleep."

Ben shut the window, then turned toward his wife, hurriedly undressing. Tomorrow was another hard day, but tonight . . . There was no curtain on the window, but that didn't matter. They were up on the second floor, and there wasn't anyone in the building adjacent to them anyway.

The next day Ben found work as a taxi driver. He'd been looking for some time. Now he and his wife would be able within a few more weeks to find a suitable and permanent place to live.

Wolf

He loved the outdoors in winter. The snow on the low sage covered hills is endless, trackless and rolling. In the open, more level areas not covered by sage, prints of grouse, quail, jackrabbit and coyote are frequent. An occasional mourning dove, often unseen, sets a melancholy tone. And when the wind is up under a blue, empty sky, blowing icy crystals of snow in sheets from the tangled, woody branches of the sage plants, a sudden pheasant explodes from this brush in a whir of labored flight and hoarse cackling. Then the sky changes and hangs like gray slate overhead, bringing in the next load of snow.

In the Salmon River Mountains to the north, the clear, cold, rushing streams run their course, hurling sprays of white water against boulders. In smoother water the light of day breaks into quivering panes of gold slipping over brown and gray stones beneath overhanging evergreen branches laden with snow. The sun melts the snow and it drips into the roaring stream. Fox come from the forest to drink, breaking the ice along the quieter pools near the edge to dip their muzzles into the chill water. The tracks of bobcat, bear and an occasional mountain lion come too, though the animals themselves are rarely seen by Ken Jordan or any other man.

Ken knew elk came down the slopes of these mountains to find winter forage among the foothills and valleys. In harsh winters he would find the carcasses of those that succumbed to the weather. Or he would find their bones already cleaned and strewn about by coyotes. When the snow was deep and held in the fastness of a twenty degree below zero cold snap, the old and the very young would starve, and mule deer would range far out into the open country and frequently be seen on his property. Pronghorn antelope would appear too, showing their precise markings, but the approach of his pickup truck would send them off swift and silent to disappear among low rolling hills. A magpie would arrive, settle on a fence, then glide off into a rocky draw, where a few small species of deciduous trees fought for a living against wind, cold, heat and drought, and where a stream ran only in spring weather.

Ken Jordan worked a small ranch where he ran beef cattle. It was not small in acreage but in the size of herd it supported. In the northern desert of the Great Basin it takes a good amount of land to support a steer. Normally Ken brought fodder out to his cattle several times a week in his pickup truck in severe weather. This would sustain them till the snow melted. But when the snow was deep, it was a struggle to reach them even on horseback. Still he came, using extra horses and pulling hay on a sled. Because of his diligence, his losses were always few, and, fortunately, the winters of southern Idaho were not so severe as those in Montana.

One winter a pack of gray wolves suddenly appeared in southern Idaho. They came down that winter out of the Salmon River Mountains, perhaps originally from Canada by way of Montana or northern Idaho, and were spotted by ranchers in groups of three, four and sometimes five. Five they commonly judged to be the full extent of individuals in the pack. Though no cattle had been taken— the calves from the previous spring were large and no easy prey— many of the ranchers began to fear for the next calving season. "Where there are five wolves, there will be more," they said to each other, nodding their heads, drawing their lips tight, and spitting on the ground.

Like the others, Ken began carrying a rifle whenever he was out on his land. He did not automatically hate or fear the wolves as many of the others did. He just wasn't taking any chances with his animals. If he saw one, he decided, he would shoot it. It was better to be safe now, rather than sorry later.

It was after a hard snow that stayed on the ground. It had lain there several feet deep for three days with no sign of thawing. The sky did not open up to sun and blue but hung low and gray. The wind was cold and bitter, whipping gusts of snow up into thin, whirling streamers that it hurled over the crystal white laden, gray green sage. White on the ground and gray above in the sky. Ken led a team of horses pulling a sled loaded with bales of hay. The sled moved well enough where he avoided the thick, tangled, woody sage, and the horses pulling it were work animals, very strong. But his relatively slender, sorrel mount found the deep snow unpredictable and was unsure of its footing.

Ken took the sled down into a draw, where the cattle often gathered when the wind was strong, and began spreading the hay out in a thin line. He remained on his horse, leaning over in the saddle, cutting the bailing wire and pulling the hay from the moving sled. Several cows, already in the draw, came over to have a look, but did not approach close enough to feed. It was then Ken noticed the gray form on the ridge on the other side of the draw. It was sitting upright, looking at him, when he saw it. He pulled his rifle from behind his saddle. Not certain of what the horse's reaction would be to the loud report of the rifle, he dismounted, holding the reins. The wolf, as if in response to seeing the gun, or to seeing him dismount, crouched down on its belly, but it did not leave. Ken took careful aim. He had the wolf's left shoulder in the cross-hairs of his scope. It was an easy shot.

He began letting out a slow breath, squeezing the trigger. The wolf got up. He shifted his aim. The wolf lay down again, looking at him.

What the hell's the matter with that animal, Ken thought. He ought to run.

He steadied his sights and squeezed. The rifle went off, creating that pleasant surprise that tells the marksman he has gotten off a good shot. He heard the yelp. His bullet was a little to the right and had hit the wolf in the ribs. A lung shot. The animal rolled over, got up and disappeared over the ridge. Ken got on his horse and went to investigate.

The wolf was lying on the ground on the other side of the ridge, panting. It was bleeding into the snow. As Ken dismounted and approached on foot, the wolf didn't move. Perhaps in its dying it couldn't see or smell him. He finished it off at twenty yards with another shot.

At home in his living room, his wife busy in the kitchen, Ken said to her, "I shot a wolf today."

"Oh? Where?"

"Over on the west tract, just beside the draw."

"Were there any others?"

"No." Ken was silent for a moment. "First time I'd ever seen a wolf," he said. His wife was busy and didn't answer.

Ken looked at the fire that was drying the wet socks still on his feet. I wonder where the others were, he thought. He fell asleep in his chair, thinking about wolves somewhere in the forest, lapping water in the dark night out of an icy stream.

Three Friends

"A civilization is measured by the character of its people," he said. The three of them were sitting at a little wooden table near the bay window of a small breakfast cafe on University Avenue in Seattle.

"That all depends on what you mean by character," the young woman said. Five foot five and shapely with short strawberry blond hair, she was the desire of both young men who presently accompanied her. The three of them were friends, two of them frequent classmates in the History Department at the University of Washington.

"I mean the temper of a people as a whole. Their tastes, attitudes . . ." Tom continued.

"What about individual moral character?" Vicki asked.

Dietrich laughed. A German foreign student enrolled in pre-medical studies at the same university, he always found the inflated intellectual conversation of American college students amusing.

"What's so funny about that?" Vicki asked. She looked offended.

"Nothing, Miss Victoria," Dietrich said. He put his hand on one of hers, which she withdrew from the table. A bus pulled up noisily, screeching its brakes on the opposite side of the street. It exchanged passengers with the sidewalk, then rumbled off headed north.

Vicki looked at the bus through the window, blushing. "Mind your manners," she said almost in a whisper.

"Yes ma'am." Dietrich was still smiling.

"Knock it off," Tom said.

"Knock off something. What?" Dietrich asked, thickening his accent and feigning ignorance, while smiling at his friend. He looked around the room for something to knock off of something.

"What you're doing."

"I think the quality of a civilization is measured by its manners. Good manners!" Vicki said emphatically.

"Oh baloney, Miss Victoria. The Romans had bad manners and they were a great civilization."

"How do you know their manners weren't good?"

"It isn't polite to feed Christians to lions."

"Depends on your view of Christians," Tom said.

"Ha ha ha. So what's your view, Thomas?"

"It isn't funny," Vicki said.

"Yes, one of my ancestors was fed to the lions," Dietrich said. He solemnly drank his glass of milk and finished his sweet roll. "She was a distant grandmother on my father's side," he added.

Tom and Vicki looked at Dietrich.

"So was she a Christian?" Tom asked. He grinned, glancing over at Vicki.

"I don't know. She couldn't read or write, so she didn't leave a diary."

They all laughed. Dietrich got up from the table. "See you guys," he said. "I'm late for class." He hurriedly picked up his books and went out the glass door of the cafe. Vicki and Tom watched him cross the street, then go out of sight around a corner, headed for the university campus. Dietrich was tall, slender and good looking with sandy hair and gray eyes. Vicki seemed lost in thought as she watched him go around the corner. The early morning sun shone through the plate glass window beside her into her pale green eyes and onto her green and white patterned blouse. The blouse was of a simple cut, wide in the neck, and hung loose and open on her shoulders. One of Vicki's white bra straps was exposed on her soft, round, faintly freckled shoulder near the lovely protrusion of her collar bone. She was beautiful.

"You like Dietrich, don't you, even though he acts cavalier?" Tom said.

"I don't know."

Tom looked at his female friend. He would've given anything to be in Dietrich's place.

Vicki turned back toward him. "You didn't really mean that about Christians, did you?" she asked, looking at him.

"Well, some Christians . . ." Tom was embarrassed. He knew Vicki was a devout churchgoer and he didn't want to offend her.

Vicki smiled. "That's okay. I know some of us don't bring much credit on the faith." She blushed. She was thinking about Dietrich again. "I don't know why he affects me like that," she said abruptly, looking out the window and across the street.

"Who?"

"Dietrich." She looked back at Tom.

"Oh. Yeah. I wish he didn't."

Vicki dropped her eyes. "I wish he didn't too," she said quietly.

"You wouldn't let him . . . seduce you, would you?"

"What kind of a question is that?"

"I'm sorry."

They looked at each other across the little table. It was of a light wood construction mounted on a wrought iron pedestal and rocked when either one of them leaned on it. Tom was dark haired, heavy browed, stocky of build, studious. The morning sunlight glinted on the lenses of his dark framed glasses.

Vicki had the greatest respect for Tom's mind. A man should be appreciated for his mind, she thought. And a good mind is more than brilliant. It has character, breadth, subtleties that are reflected in the way a person behaves. Tom has a good mind. Then she thought of Dietrich and felt a disturbing warmth. It seemed to intensify the sunlight coming through the window, and the window glass itself was giving off heat. She smiled feebly at Tom. "I'd better get to class," she said.

Tom watched her go. He wished he knew what he could do to have the same effect on her that Dietrich had. He saw a young couple coming toward him on the sidewalk on the same side of the street as the cafe. They had their arms around one another and seemed lost in each other. He tried to imagine himself and Vicki in such a way. What he saw was Vicki and Dietrich. It's inevitable, he thought. He sighed, picked up his books and left the cafe.

Differences

The spring rain was cold and beat in sheets against the narrow windowpane. Water rolled in waves down the glass and made it opaque. You could not even make out the large maple with its paired, buff colored, winged crop of seeds already falling in the yard across the street.

Tanya was in the attic of her wood frame, two story house in Woodlynne, New Jersey. Woodlynne is a Philadelphia suburb, a small community of older homes on quiet, tree lined streets near the first stop of the Philadelphia commuter train coming out of Camden. In fact, it is near a large, green, parklike cemetery that contains a duck pond and Walt Whitman's tomb. Tanya loved the peaceful calm of the cemetery but only went there with her parents.

"Tanya, come on. Mom says your eggs are getting cold." David, Tanya's younger brother, stood on the attic stairs, his burr head and square shoulders just above the floor level of the attic. "Aren't you even dressed yet?"

Tanya was in her nightgown. She often spent time in the attic alone, writing or with a book. "I'm coming," she said, gathering up pen and paper from the small desk where she sat. She pulled a long string cord to switch off the electric light bulb above her head.

"Morning, honey," Tanya's mother said cheerfully, as her daughter entered the kitchen still in her nightgown and a robe. "Planning on getting up today?"

"It's Saturday, Mom." Tanya looked at her mother with intense blue eyes. Her face had fresh color from the cold water she'd splashed on it from the bathroom sink. "Where's Dad?"

"He's out in the garden," David said.

"In the rain?"

"Well, as your father puts it," her mother said, stacking hot waffles on a platter beside the stove and pausing, "There's only one Saturday in the week, *no matter what the weather is.*" She imitated her husband's deep voice with the final clause of her quote.

Tanya laughed.

"He wanted to get the soil turned," her mother continued.

"You were going to help him with the planting," David said to Tanya.

Tanya made a face. "I didn't know it was going to rain."

"A little rain won't hurt you!" The kitchen door leading to the back yard opened and banged shut. Tanya's father stood inside the doorway, dripping wet in a brown plastic windbreaker and boots. He took off his cap and the windbreaker and hung them on a hook beside the door.

Tanya's mother set a saucer and a cup of steaming coffee on the kitchen table. "You must be freezing, Jack."

"That rain's got a chill to it," he said. "There's a wind blowing it in gusts mostly from the east. It's like a shower of needles." He passed his big hand over his son's close-cropped head as he came to the table. He looked at his daughter. "Planning on getting dressed today, young lady?"

Tanya looked down, suddenly burst into tears, and left the room.

"What's wrong with her?"

"You know full well what's wrong with her, Jack. Couldn't you speak a little more gently to your daughter? She doesn't understand why you harp on her so much."

"Well, if she'd . . ." Jack picked up his hot coffee and drank half the cup in a single gulp. Tanya's mother always watched in silent wonder as he did this. She couldn't understand how he kept from burning out the inside of his mouth. The thick index finger of his ham fist barely fit through the delicate handle of the china cup. Jack always drank from one of these cups with his little finger extended. When he did this in public, it embarrassed his wife. To her he looked like a bull eating French pastry.

"I know," Tanya's mother said. "She's in her own world. But who knows what might come of it. She's brilliant, makes good grades in school, and is quite creative. I've read some of her stories. They're good for a sixteen year old."

"That's all she ever does," David said, "sitting up there in the attic, dreaming all day." There was a general sympathy between David and his father. They were a lot alike.

After breakfast, Tanya's father knocked on the door of her bedroom. His wife had sent him upstairs to make amends. When his daughter didn't answer, he opened the door. Tanya was lying across her bed, still in her nightgown. She was a frail, slender blond, much like her mother when she was a girl. Jack had known his wife since they were children. He was often struck by this resemblance. Tanya's mother had also been a quiet, dreamy girl. "Get up, young lady," he said.

Tanya got up sniffling, wiping her eyes with her hand.

Knock off the sniveling nonsense, Jack wanted to say. But something touched his heart. He just stood and looked at her as she went over to her dresser and pulled out her clothes, keeping her back to him, her narrow white shoulders in the yellow nightgown held up in defiance of the world. He quietly shut her bedroom door.

Later in the day Jack showed his daughter where he wanted the garden seeds planted. He had the future plants arranged neatly in rows with furrows dug between them. The soil was rich and black, smelling of loam and still moist from the rain, while the sun was out with only a few white puffs of clouds in the sky. Jack and his daughter accomplished a great deal that afternoon but, as usual, without much conversation.

The Atrium

It was rush hour, somewhere between five and six in the evening. People were streaming through the heavy glass and metal doors, down the quick flights of steps and along the interminable gray carpeted halls of the underground concourse located beneath the Rainier building and adjacent areas of Seattle's business district. Young girls—secretaries and clerks—flowed along on fast, pretty legs, wearing inflexible expressions of intent. Ignoring the surrounding, expensive, subterranean shops, they were determined to get home, where the pleasure of living could begin. Few of them made sufficient income to do much. All of them looked as fragile as a sheet of rain in strong wind, which is what they were coming out of and going back into on the streets of the city above.

Out of this anxious, moving stream of young humanity stepped three souls, no less fragile in their way than the rest. Yet they were different. They were not clerks or secretaries. They were inhabitants of the street, dwellers of nowhere, disembodied and invisible in the minds of those who surged past and beyond them in the stream, yet clothed in the same physical hunger, sexual ache and psychological loneliness of all human flesh. They were an old man, hunched in the shoulders beneath a massive, rumpled black cloak, a freckled young slip of a girl insufficiently protected from the winter cold and dampness, and a boy of no more than fifteen, painfully thin but strikingly nervous and alert.

They proceeded out of the crowd and down an extra flight of steps to an old, black, baby grand piano which was situated in the middle of an atrium, its top already raised for casual use. The girl seated herself comfortably, propped on one leg, on one of several large buff-colored cushioned stools lining the walls. These were the only other furniture in the room. She wore blue jeans cut off at the ankles and patched in the rear. Her blouse, missing buttons and damp from the cold misting rain outside, was simply tied at the waist. Her ash blond hair fell in wet strands to her shoulders, tangled and unwashed. She may have been as old as sixteen, maybe less. Her breasts may have been small, her hips slender, from malnutrition.

The old man and the boy proceeded directly to the piano. The boy sat down on the long cushioned bench and lifted the varnished wood cover off the black and white keys. He sat for a moment, looking affectionately at them, as though they might have been precious jewels and he spontaneously caressing them with his heart. This attitude could be seen as well in the fond expression of the girl who watched him. It could also be felt in the stooped and studied silence of the old man who stood next to him. The old man, with his matted gray locks and oversized overrun scuffed wingtipped shoes, looked for all his misery like a dignified elderly maestro fallen on hard times. And such he must have been, for, the old man having uttered a few words in the boy's ear, the young man obediently began to play.

His long, slender, feminine fingers ran effortlessly up and down the scales. The crowd streamed on, one flight of stairs above them, paying no heed. The impoverished maestro, gesturing privately to him, instructed the boy in some mystical elements of the performance that was about to begin. The girl watched, her careful breathing discernible beneath the knot of her blouse.

The boy stopped playing the scales. He sat in silence before his instrument. The shuffle of footsteps, a chatter of voices passing overhead could again be heard. In this movement of humanity fleeing the numbing rigors of uncreative work was a sound, perhaps imagined, like a drawn breathing, the labored exertion of escape. Into that silence, like a measuring pole plunged into a tankard of oil, the boy put his fingers. Lightly, more softly than a blossom dropping scent upon a breeze, he touched the smooth keys. He leaned into them.

The atrium exploded into sound. The maestro rocked back upon his worn heels, displaying a broad grin. He exchanged a delighted glance with the girl. The boy played on, head bent, thin shoulders compressed, immersed in his music. His fingers flurried and climbed, hands arching over and under some invisible current, like a rippled movement of schooling fish. He was playing Tchaikovsky's *Concerto No. 1* in B-flat minor, playing it as no one else could have done, save as Tchaikovsky himself would have formed it in his mind while composing it. For the boy was playing from his heart.

On the open, encircling floor two flights above, all around the atrium, leaning against the rails in mobbed, gazing silence, stood a crowd which had suddenly assembled, nearly emptying the halls. When the boy finished, they burst into applause.

The Inheritance

She had been indiscriminate in her youth and the effects were clearly marked upon her body: a prematurely lined face; an unusual dryness of the skin; the limp, dull character of her hair. She kept her blond hair tightly wound in a bun. Day in and day out at home she wore an old housecoat perpetually in need of a wash and mending. Her hands were gnarled. Her breasts sagged, the nipples and areola large above her stomach, which was still flat. For she was thin.

Yet Veronica Lake had charm. Amidst the cigarettes and alcohol, the innumerable men who had passed in and out of her life, was a certain nobility. It was the instinctive pride of one who had been given the capacity for insight and thought, though it had been abused.

"Auntie. Auntie Beronka, catch!" Jonathan, her three year old great nephew, threw the ball. Veronica turned her head toward him as the rubber ball bounced off her shoulder. She laughed.

"Jonathan! You mustn't do that. Naughty boy. Poor Auntie."

"I'm fine," Veronica said smiling at her niece. She picked up her iced tea out on the cool suburban patio surrounded by a billow of intense green lawn. She closed her eyes. The breeze felt good. "When will Reggie be home?" she asked.

"I don't know," Margery answered. "He isn't usually this late." The sound of the front door closing just then could be heard from within the house. "That must be him now." Margery went into the house.

Veronica, with her eyes still closed and leaning back in the lounge chair, let the sun lay on her face like a soft, warm cloth.

"Aunt Veronica! Oh my dear aunt." Reggie pushed his muscular, six foot two frame past the open glass door onto the patio and seized his aunt's small body, lifting her out of the lounge chair in a profound hug.

"Oh, Reggie. Oh. Be careful. I'm not as strong as I used to be. I'm not a rag doll." Veronica was both laughing and moaning.

"It's been so long since I've seen you," Reggie exclaimed. "I could hardly believe it when Mom wrote and said you were coming."

"Well, I'm here. So please let me live a little longer," Veronica said, laughing again. Then, almost in a whisper, "You wouldn't have anything with a little more kick in it than this?" She held up the half empty tea glass.

"Sure." Reggie went into the house. His wife was in the kitchen. He reached into the white painted oak cabinet above the sink and pulled out a bottle of Scotch whisky, pouring a little into the bottom of a tall glass. Then he filled the glass from the tap and dropped two ice cubes into the amber liquid. They bobbed up and down.

"You know your mother says that stuff is killing her," Margery said. She was seasoning several steaks, pounding them flat on the counter with a wooden mallet.

"I know." Reggie went back out onto the patio.

Veronica took the glass, propping her elbow on the blue and yellow chaise longue chair. "Thank you, dear nephew," she said. "Thank you, dear sweet little Reggie. You take good care of your poor old aunt." The glass was already frosted from the ice. It felt cool in Veronica's hand. She closed her eyes, took a long drink and leaned back on the lounge, her eyes closed, her right arm extended with the glass in it. She looked very sensuous.

"I'm not so little any more," Reggie said. "And you're not so old. You're still a fine looking woman, Aunt Veronica."

"And you're still a flatterer. Even as a little boy, you could knock a lady over with your compliments."

Reggie didn't answer. He looked at his aunt. She had always been special to him and he loved her in a way words couldn't describe.

"And I'm not so poor either, Reggie," Veronica continued. "I've stashed quite a bit away through the years. Made some lucky investments." She propped herself up on her elbow, facing him. Reggie knew she had something important to tell him, so he squatted down close beside her. "I've come to you now for a reason. I don't want you to fret. You know how I hate such things. Blubbering and oil dripping from the eyelids. Just listen to me, dearest." She put her hand on the back of his head and kissed his forehead. "I never had a son." She leaned back. "I'm leaving you everything."

"What do you mean, Aunt?"

"Just what I said. Now, no blubbering. Be a good fellow and go get me a refill right away."

In the kitchen Reggie knew his aunt was telling him she was leaving him for good. She was dying. There were plenty of reasons for that. He knew most of her physical problems.

Back out on the porch, he simply said, "I love you, Aunt Veronica." There were tears in his eyes.

"I know you do, Reggie," she said taking the drink. "We've always been close." She paused, drinking. "There's something more I wanted to tell you. You have a mind. A good mind. I'm also leaving a large library to you. I've never read many of the books. I regret that. I always meant to. Just never did. Never found the time." Veronica looked long and quietly at her nephew. "I hope you will," she said in an almost imperceptible voice.

In the morning Veronica took a plane to Chicago, where she lived. Within a few weeks she checked into a veterans hospital. She had been an army nurse during the Vietnam War. She died of kidney failure on a quiet Sunday afternoon.

The Awakening

Darlene got up at five forty-five and lit the gas stove. The burner, which was old, had to be ignited with a match as opposed to simply using a pilot light. She put a kettle on to boil.

At six o'clock Darlene's mother got up and removed the kettle from the burner, turning off the gas jet. Then she went in and awoke Darlene's sixteen year old daughter.

"Get up, lazy bones."

"Lazy bones to you, Grandma." The girl turned her face to the wall, her brown tresses tangled on the pillow. "Ow! Don't pull my hair."

"Well, get up, Missy."

Missy was a slightly built, frail looking girl with dark brown eyes that drew you into her. "Oh, all right. You're such a tough old biddy."

"Don't you call me a biddy, young lady!" The older woman laughed and went out of the room.

*   *   *

Darlene was drinking her cup of instant coffee when Missy came to the table. A pale beam of early morning sunlight fell through the kitchen window, passing through some gossamer strands of Grandmother's thinning gray hair, then flooding from the kitchen window and sink over to the kitchenette table where Darlene sat. It put the room in a half light, since only the kitchen area light was on.

"Morning, Mom." Missy kissed the top of her mother's head as she walked into the kitchen. She was medium height with small, well articulated features. In this she closely resembled her mother, but the loose, girlish, even boyish, fit of her school clothes did not. Grandmother brought over a plate of eggs and toast, the preparation of which had filled the room with a thick smell of fried butter.

Darlene, who was glancing through a magazine, looked up and smiled. Beside her was a saucer with several half slices of toast on it, one of them partially eaten.

"Good morning, honey. Please don't forget to comb your hair this morning."

"Mom."

"Yes." Darlene had returned to her magazine and had a mouth full of toast.

"You remember John Sypes, don't you?"

"Of course I do, dear. He used to mow our lawn a few years back, didn't he?"

"He says he's got you for senior English this year."

"Oh, yes. As a matter of fact he does."

"How could you forget?"

"I didn't. I just wasn't thinking. Besides, its the beginning of the year and I do have more than one student."

"He wants to take me out Friday night."

"What!" Grandmother came over from the sink and laid a soft, wet hand on Missy's forehead. Her mother looked at her.

"Yep. She's got a pulse," Grandmother said.

"Oh, cut it out, Grandma!"

"Well, you can't go out with a young man if you don't comb your hair. And a little makeup wouldn't hurt. You're as pale as boiled beef."

"Mother, please. Don't rib her so much. Missy, what is this sudden interest?"

"It's nothing. He just asked me out, that's all."

"Well."

"Well what, Mom?"

"Well, I reckon you're old enough. I had just begun to think . . ." She paused, looking her daughter over with heightened interest, as if seeing her in a new way. It is true that she's pretty, she thought. I just hadn't considered it.

* * *

While Missy was in the bathroom washing her face, Grandmother sat down at the table. "She's unformed," she said bluntly.

"She's sixteen years old, mother."

"She doesn't have any breasts or hips."

"She doesn't need them just yet."

"You know what I mean."

"Yes, I know what you mean, Mother. I'm just as surprised as you are. I had begun to think she wasn't going to show any interest in boys at all. But she is older than a good many girls who are dating regularly now."

"She seems a mere child."

"We're all children, Mother."

"Well, your father and I were mature enough to stay together for thirty-five years."

"Mother, we've been through that. Sam and I just didn't work out. He didn't want responsibility."

"So how do you know this John does?"

"They're not getting married. Shhh."

The bathroom door, which tended to stick, could be heard opening, and Missy walked through the living room into the dinette area of the kitchen.

"Well, you do look fresh this morning, dear!" her mother said to her. "What have you just done with your hair, Missy? I like it."

"I pulled it back, Mom."

Grandmother frowned, but she was not at all certain she disapproved.

Two Brothers

The two brothers had not seen each other in three years. Terrence Crawford, a slender youth of twenty-one, had joined the Marines out of high school. He had served nearly two years of stateside training and duty, then put thirteen months in Vietnam. There he had seen his best friend, Tom Baxter, killed in action but had never shown an inclination afterward to talk much about it with anyone. Now he was home on an extended leave, deciding whether or not to reenlist.

Robert, his nineteen year old brother, had finished one year at the University of Washington. Slender and blond like Terrence, he was not quite as tall and lacked some of the muscular tone that seemed to emanate from Terrence. He was studying to become a game biologist.

"I'm planning on transferring to the University of Idaho next year," he said early one morning on a fishing trip the two brothers took together. He was bent over looking for a silver spinning lure in the tackle box they'd brought with them.

"Try that spoon," Terrence said glancing over his shoulder and pointing to a lure lying in an upper compartment. "I got a good sized salmon with that one. It was somewhere near here about this time last year."

"Who'd you come out with?"

"Nobody. Just myself."

"Wish I'd come home that weekend," Robert said.

Terrence pulled his rubber waders up and picked up his fly rod. It was eight or nine feet long and made of thin bamboo. They were on the Hoh River near the Pacific Coast in Washington State. The sun was just breaking through the tops of the Douglas fir, Pacific red cedar and western hemlock on the southeast bank of the river, where it came around a bend in the trees, turning a little to the north and flowing west. The sun was white in the morning mist that hung luminescent over the chill gray-blue water.

Terrence shivered, rubbing his hands together while still holding the slender rod in the crook of one arm. The rod flexed in the sunlight as he moved his arm back and forth with the motion of his hands. He examined the green and gold feathered fly he was using to see that it was securely fastened to the line. "Gonna get a big one this time," he said smiling.

"Sure. Biggest steelhead ever taken from these waters," Robert said. "I'm going down along the bank a ways to those rocks. You heading out there toward that pool?" Robert was fishing with a spinning outfit and would not be getting into the water.

"Yeah. See you later." Terrence waded into a swirl of the icy stream. The boulders were gray above, brown beneath its transparent surface. His leg slipped into the depression of a small, dark pool and he almost lost his footing. Working his way slowly, carefully toward the middle of the river, the water nearly came up to his hips. It pressed against him, forming a dark ripple that extended in a long V downstream. He cast his line upstream toward the farther end of a sheet of still water that looked black in the shade of the tall, densely packed evergreens that crowded up to the opposite bank.

*   *   *

At around midday, the sun directly overhead in a cloudless blue sky, the two brothers were seated next to a fire in a dry, stony channel of the river where water no longer flowed. They had broken out a six pack of beer and some sandwiches which they'd already consumed. Robert sat with his bare feet up close to the fire. The flames and smoke of the fire were almost transparent but distorted anything seen through them. His shoes and socks were suspended from sticks stuck into the rocks and soil along the edge of the fire to catch its warmth, so they could dry. Looking over at his brother sitting next to him, "I've been dating Marsha," he said.

"Marsha Baxter?" Terrence, who was sitting next to Robert on his left, looked at him with surprise.

Robert took a drink from his beer can. "Yeah. Off and on for the last six months." He observed his brother. "I think it's getting kind of serious, Ter."

Terrence looked down at his feet. They were dry from the protection of the waders, which were now spread out on the rocks in the sun. Both of his hands were on the beer can setting on the ground between his legs. The aluminum can was empty, and he had been idly bending in the sides of it with his fingers.

"Something wrong?" Robert asked.

"No."

"I know she's Tom's sister," Robert went on. "It just sort of happened. We were at a party. Well, you know how things like that get started."

"Sure," Terrence said.

"Look, Terrence, I'm sorry I brought it up."

"That's okay." Terrence got up, dropped his beer can into an empty paper sack and pulled another beer out of a red and white plastic cooler. He sat down again beside his brother, opening the can. "I think Tom would like it," he said flatly.

"Sure," Robert said. "I was hoping you'd say that." He looked away down the river toward a grove of dark green alder mixed with young, light green willow, both not more than five feet in height, growing on a sandbar where the stream flow temporarily divided. A raccoon had come out onto the near shore of the sandbar and was fingering the rocks in shallow water. "Look!" Robert pointed. "Must be looking for crayfish."

"Or mayfly nymphs." Terrence picked up a stone and threw it into the water. The raccoon looked up, its sensitive brown eyes glancing nervously left and right through its black mask, then it backed out of sight into the brush.

"What did you do that for?"

"I don't know." Terrence paused, squinting his eyes in the bright sunlight as he looked up at the tall evergreen treetops for a moment. "Robert, when Tom got it over there, I was with him."

"I know that."

"We were ambushed and he wasn't the only one hit. But I was with him . . . when he died."

Robert looked carefully at his brother.

"He said," Terrence continued, "that I should look after Marsha. You know I used to have an interest in her."

Robert nodded without answering.

Terrence took a drink from his beer can. He drew his cheeks in from the coldness of the liquid and swallowed. It made his teeth ache. "It's okay," he said, looking into the fire. "I told you I thought Tom would approve."

Robert appeared visibly relieved. He stood up and got another beer, then walked barefoot over the smooth, dry, white rocks to the water's edge. The water rushed cheerfully, noisily downstream, where the whitecaps shone in the sun. Squatting down, he tugged at something under the water and pulled out three large trout attached to leaders. "You did good," he said, shouting back to his brother. Then he set the fish back into the water, still fastened with fishing line to a stake on shore. They moved sluggishly together under the surface, like a triple brace of old horses.

* * *

That evening in the growing twilight, the two young men drove along a winding paved road that followed the eastern shoreline of Lake Crescent. The sun was setting well behind the trees, casting the road into darkness. In their headlights, they caught sight of a deer alongside the road. As they approached, the deer stepped in front of them, its eyes glowing in the headlights. Robert applied the brakes. The old pickup truck shuddered to a stop and stalled. Robert cursed. The deer stood in front of them, staring into the headlights.

"Damn fool deer!"

"It's a yearling," Terrence said. "See the spikes?"

Robert switched off the headlights, and the young animal slipped back into the forest.

At home in the dark, the two brothers clomped noisily up wooden porch steps into a warmly lit farmhouse, carrying their day's catch, rods and reels, the latter of which they deposited in the outer room. Inside was the chatter of their two younger sisters and mother. The kitchen was steamy. There was a smell of smoke in the house, sharp from green or wet logs that had been thrown into the wood burning heater. Their father was in the living room in the big armchair, asleep with a Craftsman tool catalog open on his lap.

Small Talk

She had aged beautifully. You could see her intelligence in her face. Bertram, who was three years older than his sister and looked more his age, attributed her fine appearance, above all, to the development of her mind and spirit. Of course, her figure also remained firm and shapely, her skin smooth like a child's, but he was certain, in this case, that inner character governed the outer form.

Bertram himself was a bit of an odd figure. Muscular, a little hairy and lithe at fifty with long drooping hairs on prominent brow ridges, he was nevertheless markedly stooped in the shoulders and reclusive and withdrawn in his habits to the point of eccentricity. He had been a laboring man all his life but, through extensive reading, had become profoundly, if somewhat erratically, educated.

At forty-seven Denise had come home to the house where Bertram now lived and where they had both grown up. It was an old two story white clapboard house with a bit of undeveloped land about it in the sandy pine barrens of southern New Jersey. Their parents were gone and Denise, recently divorced, had no children.

"What will you do now?" Bertram asked his sister. They were out in the poultry yard one morning where Bertram was feeding a varied assortment of mixed breed chickens, ducks and turkeys. There were no geese. He hated geese for their nasty dispositions.

"I think I should be able to find a teaching position here."

"Don't know as anybody around here much cares about English or literature," he said.

"Their children still have to learn it in school." Denise paused.

Bertram, in his usual stooped manner, was scattering cracked corn poultry feed on the ground from a large coffee can he was holding in one massive hand. He made a chirring sound with his tongue behind his teeth as he did so. A mottled assortment of brown, black, gray, red, speckled and tan chickens of all sizes, ages, sex and descriptions ran up and began pecking furiously at his feet. He was wearing heavy leather boots which they fluttered to avoid as he stepped back and forth, distributing the contents of the can. Several ducks, one white, two mallards, wandered over. A turkey stood nearby, gazing with one cocked imbecile eye upon the busy scene. The morning breeze was softly cool and sweet through the surrounding scrub pine forest. The sun, seen in glimpses through the trees, was up full and yellow in the clear eastern sky.

"Bert, would you mind terribly if I stayed with you for awhile? I . . . well, after the divorce my finances are a little strained."

"No, of course not," Bert answered, looking up from the chickens. "This is your home too. Always has been."

Denise smiled and, taking her brother's arm, while relieving it of the emptied coffee can with her free hand, went back into the house with him.

Perhaps Denise's good looks were at fault, but there were always those in the nearby town of Sharpsville who had certain suspicions and wagged their heads and clicked their tongues accordingly. For many years it had been their theory that, because he had never married, Bertram Walker must be a homosexual. But some of the older folks in town remembered how close Bertram and Denise had been in their growing up years. Why, there had even been a certain amount of talk concerning them back then. It wasn't natural for a brother and sister to spend so much time together, especially in their teens. They were always discussing, it seemed, arcane subjects like literature, philosophy and science that hardly anyone understood. Then, when Denise had gone off to college and subsequently married some young lawyer from Cincinnati, Ohio, Bertram had become the semi-recluse he was today, living out his years alone in his parents' home until they had recently passed away. Now Denise was back, twice divorced. It seemed neither had ever been able to love another person successfully.

"Denise," Bert said one morning coming downstairs. Denise was dusting in the large dining area near the stairwell. She had been back about a year. "I overheard some talk at the hardware store."

Denise looked up at her brother. He had that careworn look he always had when people became a problem. She laid the duster on the dining room table. A rich mahogany, the table shone under a fine English polish. "I don't care," she said. She paused. "I know what they're saying."

Their eyes met, and they stood looking at each other for a moment. In that moment the combined fortitude of brother and sister rose up against the townspeople and then subsided in gentleness.

"People are foolish," Denise said, returning to her dusting. The smell of pine oil from the kitchen floor mingled with the mellower scent of furniture polish. In the old house there was a sense of substantiality, of familiarity, of durability from these clean household odors which had been routine ingredients of their housekeeping from childhood. Outside a rooster crowed.

"I'd better tend to old Hornblower's harem," Bert said grinning.

"Yes, you tell him if those lady friends of his don't start coming up with more eggs, the whole darned lot of them are going to find themselves in a considerable stew!"

Bertram went clumping out the door laughing. Denise, smiling, went on with her dusting. The china cabinet, which she had earlier wiped down with oil, and which was of the same rich brown mahogany tone as the large table, was so lovely! The polished wood was glassy smooth. She could almost see her reflection in it. In this simple place where she had grown up, and where all things were intimately familiar, including the ungracious talk of some of their neighbors, she had found an indescribable peace overall.

Coming into Focus

She had been a sensitive child, and this had given her a naive, or guileless, quality, which she learned to conceal in adolescence. Then early womanhood had brought about a further adjustment of the social mask she had designed for herself. She attained to a more perfect fit, in the external impression she made, with an appropriate adornment in dress, makeup and carefully chosen ornaments. Even such decisions as how many buttons to leave undone at the neckline of her blouse or at what point to suspend the hemline of her skirt were considered crucial. A delicate balance must be maintained in her relations with other women and with men. They must think her at all times fresh and vital, but never wanton.

In this state of mind and development of personal architecture, or at least the scaffolding of it, which she never thought to take down, Patricia Somers met her man, fell in love and married. He, of course, did not really know her. He married what he saw. She bore him children, three in five years. He was an electrician, insensitive, simple. His principal role at home seemed to be to flail about upon her stomach for short intervals to produce another child. However, three were quite enough, thank you.

At any rate, he was often away for weeks or months at a time. His longest contract to date was six months spent on the North Slope in Alaska. Something to do with the pipeline, or with housing for those who worked on it, or with bringing in power for the equipment. Well, something. They rarely discussed his work in detail.

"Pat, I think you should get out more. Get away from the kids. Fred and I can watch them. It'll do you a world of good." Marsha

Davidson was sitting on the wooden steps of Patricia's white, chipped-paint porch. She held a simple, gray, undecorated, stoneware tea cup in her hand. Patricia did the same from a rocking chair by the front door.

"I don't know," Patricia said. She took a sip of the warm brew and held it in her mouth, rocking, ruminating. "I wouldn't know what to do."

"You can think of something. What'd you do before you were married? Take in a movie. Go into town to the Mall. Join a club. I don't know." Marsha paused, looking at her friend and neighbor. "The point is, Jack has no right to leave you alone so much of the time. And when he is home, what does he do? He goes fishing with his old high school buddies. You would think he would've grown up by now. You've been married near fifteen years."

Marsha set her tea cup down on one of the wooden steps, which were painted a drab brown and scuffed to almost no color at all, and took a hard look at her friend. She knew her advice was dangerous. She had come to know Patricia perhaps better than anyone. That plain little woman in the simple frock dress was not who she seemed, even to herself. She was burning inside, and Marsha knew it. If she let herself go, who knew where it might lead? It could destroy Patricia's marriage, her family. It could even lead to terrible loneliness and hard trials. But where was dear Pat now? In a cage of her own sweet making. And Jack, her bozo of a husband, had locked the door on it.

"I tell you what," Marsha said. "Fred and I are going out for a little fun this Saturday. A little country dancing and beer at the Red Kettle. Want to come?"

"No. I . . . I can't. Who would watch the kids anyway?"

"Your oldest can handle it. Besides, my Priscilla can look in on them. And if there's any kind of a problem, they can just give her a yell."

"Jack … "

"Never mind Jack. He's been gone two weeks and only called once." Marsha might have added that she doubted Jack was keeping himself as lonely as his wife was, but she didn't have the heart.

In the end, Patricia went with the Davidsons to the country pizza bar. There were peanut shells on the floor, and the communal tables and benches were made of long, rough wooden planks. The interior was semi-dark and everyone was dressed in country garb, or most everyone. The large, rectangular room, with a long bar on one wall and a kitchen on the other, smelled of beer, cigarette smoke and baking pizza. Outdoors at seven o'clock the evening sun was still warm.

Patricia wore a simple blue denim halter, thin black cotton slacks and felt absolutely naked. Men noticed her immediately upon entering the room because she was still a very shapely redhead in her mid-thirties, and soon one of them asked her to dance. He was a pleasant, handsome fellow with a disarming sense of humor, so they quickly fell to exchanging friendly repartees on the dance floor, laughing at one another's responses.

Patricia returned to her table flushed. She felt excited and frightened. She wanted to go home.

"Nonsense," Marsha responded when she had intimated her desire. "It's not yet even dark out."

"But my children …"

"They're fine! Relax!"

Patricia had another beer and another after that. Now she could hardly stand up, and the handsome fellow wanted to dance again. She went out to the dance floor. It was a slow number. They danced very close, until Patricia thought she would faint. She felt warm in places she shouldn't. Very warm. And weak. She wanted to give in to the flow of the moment and be carried away by it.

Back at the table, Patricia kept insisting upon leaving, until the Davidsons begrudgingly obliged and took her home. She was in bed by nine o'clock and slept for ten hours.

In the morning Patricia had a headache and drank water. Then she felt dizzy. She searched her memory. She had done nothing irreparably wrong. Sipping cold instant coffee at the breakfast table, she tried to think it over. At quarter after seven, her children were still asleep.

First of all, she didn't really know herself, she concluded. This was clear. She had decided she wanted to really live her life. Oh, how she wanted to live it! And she knew it for a certainty now. No more empty, meaningless days. But then, what did it mean to want to live? That was not clear. That was something she would have to work out over time.

As she sat at the table, head in her hands, coffee cup placed before her, now ignored, Patricia tried to form in her mind a clear picture of her husband, her three children and herself. It was the one of herself which seemed fuzziest, the hardest to focus. Yet it was easier to concentrate on that one than the others. It was all very confusing and frightening.

The Reading Club

As a successful novelist he had no complaints. A few more critics swept into the dustbin of history couldn't help but improve matters, but otherwise he felt good about that portion of his life. He had succeeded in his professional endeavors. A bachelor, he also owned a pleasant third floor flat on the Upper East Side of Manhattan. It was, of course, tastefully decorated. He was fifty-three years of age, a little portly but not without his charms.

"John," he said one morning at the reading club in midtown Manhattan, "I've been seeing a lady."

"Well good for you, Thomas. I had begun to lose all hope for you." John took a sip of his martini. He was a small man, approximately Tom's age, with a clean lined, close cropped, gray white beard.

"I am serious, you know. She's older than I am. Quite a bit older, in fact. But a lovely person. And well preserved, to say the least."

"Well, that's certainly important. You don't want them sagging out of the armholes of their dresses or bulging in their nylons, do you?"

"Stop being facetious. I'm not trying to be funny."

"Nor am I. It's just that I've always thought of you as a confirmed bachelor."

"Well I am. Or was. Oh, I don't know. Believe me, this is certainly new to me. I don't quite know what to make of it. I feel like a young man of twenty."

"Sap's running, huh? The dormant little beast has finally risen in the hinterland."

Tom McCarthy turned red. He felt the tingling of his own blood from head to toes and shifted uncomfortably in the plush leather armchair of the reading room. The room was fairly good sized and high ceilinged. This allowed the stacks of books on all four walls to ascend upwards in a double tier. Books bound in luxurious leather and cloth, resplendent in gold embossed majesty. A narrow, banistered walkway, approached by a polished wooden staircase, provided access to the upper level collection of books. The walkway circled the entire room above the men's heads. In the midst of the room were comfortable chairs placed strategically next to small tables with brass tops. The tables had carved legs made of a dark rosewood. It was one of these that both men set their drinks upon. The table was between their chairs. The carpet underfoot was dense, deep red, of a color to enhance richness and of a texture to suggest the impossibility of loud and unpleasant noises. The narrow, gray hustle, shout and honk between tall buildings on Forty-second Street just outside the south wall could not even be imagined from within this room.

"I'm sorry, old boy. I didn't mean to embarrass you. Care for a refill? I'm going for one." John Adams, a declared scion of the original of that name, left the room with both glasses.

This left Tom with a moment of contemplation. He thought over his predicament. His problem, which he wished to discuss candidly with his uncooperative friend, was this: He was very much attracted to Marlene Deisher. She was tall, slender, in her early sixties, a retired businesswoman, married once before. Her husband had passed away some years ago. She was a little taller than himself, in fact, and was possessed of a certain poise, a finesse of manner and speech. And she had a mind! Oh, Lord! What a luxury a mind is in any American, he thought.

But the problem lay in his long bachelorhood. Tom, for all his success and the attentions of many members of the opposite sex, had never been able to bring himself to form any close female attachments. He had never married and had formed only one liaison with a woman years before. This had culminated in a singularly disastrous attempt at lovemaking in the woman's apartment. At the crucial moment he simply hadn't been able to "get it up." The use of such a phrase embarrassed him.

Now the point was this: Was he gay? He had never felt more than a warm attachment for his male friends. But . . . they were important to him.

"Lost in thought again, Tom? I suppose you're inventing another one of those infernal novels of yours. Where do you ever get such ideas?" John handed him his refilled sherry glass and sat down with his own martini. He drank these very dry. Just a kiss of vermouth. Tom wondered how his friend ever swallowed the stuff.

"I've been thinking," John went on, having comfortably seated himself. "I thought, how can I help my old friend and club companion of these many years?" He took a sip of his martini, throwing his head back to swallow it as though he'd just bolted a shot of molten whisky. "Ahhh!" He laid his head back on the chair and closed his eyes. In this posture he continued, addressing the ceiling or upper stacks of books with his eyes still closed. "I'll get to the root of the matter. Your apparent perplexity concerning the lady in question arises, I would say, from a simple compound of inexperience and timorousness. Though, Lord knows how anyone who writes such torrid novels could be afraid of a mere flesh and blood woman." He opened his eyes and looked slyly over at his friend, for the novels were anything but torrid, though one wouldn't have guessed from them that the author knew so little about relations between men and women.

John suddenly sat bolt upright. "Look old boy, have you actually done anything yet?"

Tom reddened.

"All right, all right, perhaps the old horse is too tired to gallop anyway." He laid his head back on the chair again and closed his eyes. "I mean, if it's a platonic sort of thing you want, don't marry. I wouldn't consider..."

"Drop it, John. I was just trying to express my feelings for a delightful woman. I'll keep it to myself from now on, if you don't mind."

"Well, have it your way." John took another sip of his martini, pursing his lips. He fell asleep in his chair.

Three Generations

"I'm not wrong, Mother." Linda had come home from a bad marriage and could not make herself understood. "I didn't just leave him or get involved with Larry on a whim. It was a long time in coming."

"Your father thinks you are lowering yourself with this—this liaison of yours."

"I haven't seen Larry in several weeks, Mother. I think it's already through between us. It was just, just . . ."

"Just an affair?"

"No. Yes. Oh, who cares. Think whatever you want to. You're going to think the worst anyway."

"Linda," her mother called after her as she left the room. "Linda, I'm just trying to understand you, to understand what's happening to you and your little girl. You do have Naomi to look after, you know. Think of her. Linda. Oh, for Pete's sake. You never were any good at listening to advice." Mrs. Bonham sat down in the living room where she'd been conversing with her daughter. She heard her daughter's stereo come on in the guest bedroom where both her daughter and eleven year old granddaughter were staying. It had been Linda's bedroom to begin with, before she left home for college sixteen years ago.

The stereo clicked off again in the bedroom. Marlene thought about her daughter and how she and her husband Leonard had scrimped to give her an education.

She put her hands palm down on her knees. Her hands looked swollen, rough and wrinkled. There were age spots on them. Her legs seemed to have gotten to be too big. She'd been pretty when young, but now in her mid fifties, she felt as if she were nothing but facial lines and sagging muscles. "Maybe not that bad," she said aloud. "Leonard still loves me." She smiled. Making love to her, he could get aroused in the middle of an arctic blizzard.

She got up and went into the kitchen. Things were always better than they seemed. From the kitchen she heard the toilet flush and the shower come on. A few minutes later Linda was standing in the kitchen, dripping wet with a large white towel wrapped around her. Her hair was piled on top of her head inside another towel.

"Mom, I'm sorry."

"I know you are, honey. Things'll work out."

"I'm not just sorry for what I said. I'm sorry for the affair. I—I can't explain it. Things just built up. It wasn't until that happened that I even realized how unhappy I'd been."

"It's not just you I was thinking of, Linda. It's bad for Naomi. I mean, what must she think? Her mother having an affair with another man and leaving her father. Poor child."

"She understands, Mother. We've had a long talk about it."

"A child may appear to understand what she does not."

"I'm telling you, she understands, Mother. She was there when Dick would come home drunk from being out with his friends. She's seen him hit me and heard his foul mouth."

"He struck you?"

"Yes."

"I didn't know. You never told me."

"It's not easy talking about such things."

"Not even to your mother?"

"Would you have understood?"

"Of course. Well. Maybe not. These are such difficult times." Marlene turned toward the kitchen sink. "Leonard would never lay a hand on me." She turned on the tap. "I guess I don't realize how lucky I've been, how lucky your father and I have both been."

"I'm grateful to you, Mother, for my happy childhood. It's different for us. But Naomi will be all right. I won't ever neglect her."

"No, I don't believe you would." Marlene turned off the tap and came over and hugged her daughter.

The back entrance door to the kitchen opened and Naomi came in off the back porch, filling the room with the slightly chill but refreshing morning air of a northern spring. It came in with her as if she were wrapped in an envelope of it. The crisp air was electric with the energy of the girl herself, with the energy of chirping sparrows on sun drenched sidewalks.

"Hi Mom. Hi Grandma. Guess what."

"What?"

"Some robins have built a nest under the eaves of the garage. There are four blue eggs in it."

"If they're up there, how do you know that?" her mother asked.

"I got Grandpa's stepladder and climbed up and took a peek."

"That old wooden thing. Why, it's so old and rotted, several of the steps are missing. You be careful, young lady." Marlene looked at her granddaughter with concern.

Naomi, thin as a rail, wearing glasses, knobby kneed under a short dress, smiled at her grandmother through silver braces. She looked wide eyed with excitement and wonder, as if to ask: What could be more important than finding robin eggs on a bright, sunny morning before breakfast?

Forgiveness

They had gone to the theater and were observing a performance of Oliver Goldsmith's *She Stoops to Conquer*. The acting was superb. Hushed except for an occasional cough or burst of laughter, the room was intense with the actors' crisp dialogue. The audience was shrouded in darkness, all light being concentrated upon the small, circular, relatively bare stage.

A woman in the audience, who was in her late forties, leaned over and whispered into the ear of a man sitting next to her, "The least you could've done was to have informed me of the truth."

"I told you, Melissa," he said, raising his voice inside an answering whisper, "I didn't know until this morning at work. I never thought . . ."

"Shhh. We'll talk about it later." She pressed his hand. It was cold and clammy. He reluctantly took her left hand with the familiar ring on it and held it. It was warm, but he thought it felt a little less responsive than usual to his touch.

* * *

Outside the theater it was dark, starry, pleasant and warm, the heat of the day not yet having dissipated from the streets and sidewalks. The theater crowd was dispersing quickly into cars and taxis that pulled up regally to the curb, flashing big headlights, or they went more modestly in groups of two, three and four into the adjacent parking lot.

Barnaby Jones and his wife Melissa strolled along in the evening air. They crossed an intersection lined with rows of sleek, purring cars waiting for the light, then crossed another one at a right angle to the first. Now on a well lit street lined with glittering facades, they were able to look into various shop and display windows. A department store showed men's and women's apparel. The clothing was expensive, the ladies fabrics often gossamer, the plastic or ceramic manikins curiously attractive, even sexy.

They passed a dimly lit jewelry store, an iron gate extended and locked in front of the windows. Melissa stopped and looked at a pearl necklace with a pendant at its center. The pearls were small and lustrous, of obvious high quality in spite of their size. The pendant was of a delicate construction, its three diamonds nevertheless of a bright and generous proportion.

"Expensive," Barnaby observed. He was still holding his wife's hand. He felt as if a stone were lying in his stomach.

"But beautiful," Melissa observed.

Barnaby sighed. "Beautiful things are always expensive."

Melissa glanced up at him. He was tall, graying, handsome in middle age, the very image of a successful businessman. "Was she . . . pretty?"

Barnaby paused, fixing his eyes on the necklace, so as not to have to look at his wife. "Yes."

"Why on earth didn't you ever tell me?"

Barnaby looked at his wife. His eyes were sad. He felt ashamed. "There wasn't anything to tell. I didn't know . . ."

"She was pregnant? You might've guessed."

"I had no reason to think it, Melissa. I was on a three day in-country R and R. My best friend had just been killed. I wasn't thinking about anything. We met casually over beer in the officer's club."

"She was a nurse?"

"There were lots of young army nurses there. Civilian, as well. I'm sorry."

"It was just as much my fault, Barney. I shouldn't've stopped writing you."

"Why did you stop? I thought . . ."

"You thought I'd found someone. I hadn't. There has never been anyone but you. I just couldn't bear the waiting and worry anymore, never knowing. Every night on TV they showed the killing at Khe Sanh and in Hue City. I knew you were there somewhere, but I was no longer sure."

"Not sure you loved me?"

"No. Not sure of where you were. Not sure you were alive. I didn't want to know if you weren't. I didn't want someone showing up at my door in a starched Marine uniform to tell me you were coming home in a . . . in a . . ."

"Body bag. I know, Melissa. I wrote you as often as I could. They were moving us about in the hills outside Khe Sanh. It was pretty intense. When my platoon sergeant got it—we had become the best of friends as I said—they pulled me out of the field for three days. The colonel figured that was enough time for me to get over it." He squeezed Melissa's hand. "What I did can never be forgiven."

"It happened a long time ago, Barney. It shouldn't have happened, but it did." Melissa looked into her husband's eyes. She was built somewhat like him and looked good with him at cocktail parties and business social events, especially in a modestly revealing dress. "We have to go on. We have two fine, grown up children. We have to think of them too." Her eyes were gray and firm, her lips now compressed. Her blond hair, which hung to just above the shoulders and retained its youthful sheen and body, seemed to have only grown blonder through the years. She wore her makeup lightly over a few age lines that deepened the expression in her eyes. "I'm a stronger woman now than I was then." She paused. "And you're a stronger man. I know that."

"You can forgive me?"

"You know I do."

"It's three grown up children now," he said looking away. Though relieved, he still felt embarrassed. He didn't want to show how relieved he was, even though he'd known from the beginning she would forgive him. He had certainly lived with Melissa long enough to be aware of the courage and largeness of her character.

"Do you have her address?" she asked.

"My daughter? Yes."

"Then I think you should contact her." She squeezed his hand and smiled.

"I will," he said quietly. They were still standing in front of the jewelry store. Down the street was the parking garage where they'd chosen to leave their car.

Red Herring

On the northern tip of the Olympic Peninsula in Washington State there is a heavy cloud cover which often hangs over the town of Port Angeles. It extends along the cold waters of the Strait of Juan de Fuca beyond this small harbor and collects unbroken above Puget Sound. But it is rarely so in the strait itself, which, being at a right angle to the sound and extending from the Pacific Ocean, allows light to break through and roll back the flannel covering. A salmon, magenta and slate colored sky provides a backdrop to the dark-diving and bright-flashing white-bellied soaring of sea swallows which come in from the coast. Pacific herring flash like silver needles among the eelgrass in close packed shoals under the green waters about the wooden piles of the wharves.

A young man pauses on a wharf and looks into the water. He is observing the fish, but his mind is elsewhere. Behind him is a tall, dark green mountain range, seeming to cut him and the town off from the rest of the world.

"Where have I gone wrong?" he asks himself. A seagull cries in response. The bird lands on the wharf, cocks its head and looks at him. It takes off and circles overhead. "She shouldn't have gone home," the young man adds, continuing his monologue. "We could've worked it out. We still could. But she won't. Well, it doesn't matter."

The young man steps back from the side of the pier and walks toward the town.

* * *

It is fifteen years later. A man in his mid-thirties is seen walking slowly westward along the main street of the same town. He stops at a small, secondhand book store and buys a newspaper, then backtracks to a restaurant which is about a block and a half south of the previously mentioned pier.

Inside, at ten-thirty in the morning, the restaurant is empty. Rows of tables line either side wall. He sits on the left in the semidarkened room. His head is bent over the newspaper when a waitress comes up to him. She places a menu in front of him, catching a glimpse of his face, then steps back suddenly.

"I'll start with black coffee," the man says flatly, without pausing to look up from his newspaper.

There is no response. The man glances up dully, then wide-eyed. "Karen! Uh. I'm sorry. I was preoccupied." In a quieter voice, "How are you doing?"

There is a pause. The waitress appears to be in a trance. Then, in a tiny voice, "Okay. How about you?"

"Okay too, I guess." The man, Donald Osborne, drops his eyes. He observes the waitress' short blue skirt, its careful hem, the familiar slender legs.

The cause of this subdued verbal interchange is that these two, who were married and have not seen each other in fifteen years, have never been divorced. Karen Osborne cannot believe her eyes. This is the husband who simply vanished one day. She sits down at the little table, facing him.

"Do you mind?" she asks.

"No."

"I guess it's an obvious question," she asks, still speaking softly. "but . . . where have you been?"

"Here and there." Donald looks into Karen's eyes. "Just around," he says. "Nowhere in particular."

"Nowhere in particular!" Karen's voice rises almost to a shout. Her face reddens. Is it anger or some other emotion? Donald is looking into her blue eyes. There are lines around them and a certain hardness that waitresses have. Perhaps it's the mascara. He can see that she's not had an easy time of it.

"I went east," he says. "New York, Philadelphia. I almost went to Paris."

"Paris?"

"Well, I considered it, but I never went."

"So what did you do?"

"I worked . . . different places. Any job I could get."

"You could've written."

"You had left me."

"Not forever." She sounds almost pleading.

"I didn't know that."

For a while they sit in silence and look at each other, renewing their memory. Each seems to be trying to read the other's history in his or her face.

The restaurant owner, a large built man in his late twenties, in need of a shave and exuding an aura of uneducated cunning in both expression and manner, comes out of the rear kitchen area and addresses Karen.

"Molly needs help back there with the prep work," he says, "if you got no cause to be up front." Approaching the table, he gives Donald a harsh look. Donald stares back.

"I'm coming, Max," Karen says sharply. "Just give me a minute." She turns around and looks at him. "I work hard enough, don't I?" Max walks away toward the kitchen.

Donald is genuinely surprised at Karen's toughness. This is not the woman he left behind. She seems thin across the shoulders, a little stooped.

"Karen?" he asks. "You got anybody?"

"No. Not now." She looks candidly into his eyes.

He drops them. Though he is not innocent in this matter himself, it takes a minute to digest her response. "I won't ever ask," he says, looking up.

"Ask what?" Karen is indignant.

"Nothing. Forget it." He drops his eyes again. They sit for another moment in silence, then he gets up to leave. Karen gets up with him.

"I never got you your coffee," she says. Her voice is soft. "Want me to get it?" Her voice is caressing.

He shakes his head. "No. Some other time."

"Donald."

"Yes."

"I'm sorry I went home."

"I'm sorry too," he says, smiling. He touches her arm. She doesn't pull back. She looks at him with tears in her eyes. His also are moist.

"I'm not leaving for awhile," he says. Then he goes out of the restaurant.

High Finance

Rick Mullins had climbed the corporate ladder because he had ability. Yes, it was true. But he had also arrived at the position of junior executive at a relatively young age because of who he was, because of who his father was, because he had gone to the right schools, because he knew important people. Of course, there was always money. Not his but his father's.

Rick drove a nice car and owned a two story brick home with white Doric columns in front in a green, very quiet neighborhood. He had begun his business career in middle management—being placed there for the sake of experience—and risen by the age of thirty-five to the top floor of the corporate headquarters building. It was a floor composed of plush board rooms and comfortable offices lined with drapes, tasteful art and fine furniture.

Rick's wife was a different sort. A product of lower middle class antecedents, she had been a ballerina with a small dance company winter based in Atlanta, Georgia. The company traveled during the summer season and Rick had met June Paulsen in Pensacola, Florida, where he was then in training as a Marine fighter pilot. That was twelve years ago, and they had two children now, a boy and girl, ages ten and eight.

"June, I'm home." Rick closed the front door and stood in a spacious entranceway in front of a broad, oak banistered staircase leading to the bedrooms on the second floor.

"Mom's out back in the garden, Dad." Ten year old Ricky stood at the top of the stairs. His blond hair was uncombed, his glasses canted at about a thirty degree angle on his face. He was holding a wire cutter and a strand of small gauge electrical wire.

"You're making another mess, son?"

"No sir."

Rick smiled. He knew better.

Out in the garden beyond the patio, June was clipping flowers. Her garden gloves were covered with damp clods and wet stains from the rich black humus soil she had worked in replanting some bulbs. She was in short shorts and a yellow halter top that left her midriff and shoulders exposed. Rick looked at her for a moment from behind. June had gained a little weight from childbearing, but, as a medium height, pleasantly built redhead, she still resembled the slender, lithe dancer she'd once been.

"I'm home, June."

"Oh!" June turned around and straightened up. "I didn't hear you come in." She walked over and perfunctorily kissed her husband on the lips. "I've been busy replanting the irises and I've put some more lilies and daffodils in over there. Why so early?"

"I've something to tell you. You know we're selling off the Handy Arnold store chain."

"Yes."

"Because we overextended ourselves. We need capital."

"I know that." June set the clippers on the patio table.

"Hello June. Rick." The next door neighbor waved at June then nodded to Rick, as he passed the four foot hedge separating the two properties.

"Hi Jim." June waved back, smiling.

Jim went into his house.

"What's he want?" Rick asked.

"He's just being friendly."

"He just likes looking at you."

"Oh, Rick, don't start that."

"Well, you could wear a little more."

"I'm dressed fine."

They both paused. Rick was possessive and June could not ever forget that Rick's old, maiden, great aunts, both of them, had written into their wills that if Rick should die young—that is, while they still lived—no inheritance would then pass to his wife and children when they themselves, the aunts, passed on.

"What about selling off that chain, Rick? It's been in the works for months."

"We've got an agreement. The lawyers have to work out a few details but . . ."

"That's good, honey."

"No it isn't. It's still going to leave us in the red. Remember the other hardware chain that was doing so well, that we bought up for shares of our stock six months ago? Don Thorpe, the original owner, got so many shares he'd have controlling interest in the corporation now if he hadn't agreed to sit out and not vote or meet with the board for one year."

"I know." June was bored. She adjusted her halter top over her brassiere and brushed some dirt off her bare calf.

It was these sorts of gestures in public that troubled Rick. They were inappropriate, suggestive, he thought. Certainly his aunts weren't impressed. "Well, he found out about our secret deal to sell the whole corporation off to Martin Hannaker Trust. That means he wants to assert his right as first shareholder to prevent the deal from going through. He knows he'll lose controlling interest if we sell. Anyway, it could get legally nasty."

June looked at her husband. She had sat down on a white ironwork patio chair while he remained standing. Resting her elbow on the glass top of the matching table, she wondered if her husband was trying to tell her that their way of life was in jeopardy. She glanced at the Japanese hydrangea bush set close to the house beside the patio. A bumblebee fumbled at one of its lavender blue flowers. She felt numb to the idea. It just didn't matter. She knew they'd have enough money to live comfortably and educate the children, no matter what. "We'll be alright," she said quietly.

Rick passed a hand affectionately over his wife's soft, well rounded, bare shoulder. "Well, the price of *this* real estate won't go down," he said teasingly.

June laughed ironically. "Is that what I am to you?" she asked. "Just a piece of real estate."

Rick kissed his wife hard on the mouth. "I'm going in to fix myself a drink, dear," he said. "You want one?"

A Gift of Former Times

The two bartenders helped their familiar patron to the door. The patron, Lon Mackey, stood uncertain on his feet in the doorway. The door was open. The light was brilliant outside, the air fresh, the room dark and close within. A tink of glasses and brittle chatter came from the bar.

"Jesh one more drink," Lon insisted. Lon was a stocky, sandy haired man of medium height in his middle forties. He hadn't shaved this morning. Bracing one thick hand against the door jamb, leaning his head over his chest, stoop shouldered, swaying, he stood looking at the floor as he spoke.

"No," the youngest of the two bartenders said. A lean and muscular fellow, he was out of patience.

"Aw cmon, John. I haven't done anything. Beshides, I didn' finish my . . . , my dri . . ."

"You can finish it later."

Lon turned around reluctantly with John's help and staggered disappointedly out the door. There was a concrete platform, three feet by three feet and six inches high, in front of the door. He toppled off it like a bowling pin and lay on the ground smiling at no one in particular. Then he began to chuckle.

"He thinks he's funny," John said.

The second bartender was big, a tall, heavyset man, thick jowled, closer to Lon's age. "Look, John," he said in a low, deep voice that seemed to rumble about in his chest before escaping his mouth, "It's near time for me to get off work anyway. Why don't I just take him home?"

"Suit yourself, Frank."

"Help me get him into the car."

The two men loaded Lon into the back seat of Frank's car, which was parked directly in front of the lounge. Putting him in the back seat was like trying to lift a two hundred and ten pound sack of potatoes. It seemed as if every part of Lon was out of joint with the rest of him and had to be individually stuffed into the car.

Lon was in his own world: "Aw cmon, Marge. What's the use, honey, in getting so upset. I wasn't there, I tell you. Ummmm." He drifted off into mumbling, lying face down on the seat, his feet drawn up behind him, almost in a fetal position. His blue eyes looked sick, as if they had a film over them.

The two bartenders stood back from the rear door of the car, looking at Lon and wondering if he was going to vomit. They were wearing immaculately clean, freshly pressed, white aprons with the lounge's logo embroidered in red and gold thread on them. The name of the lounge was the Gilded Jaguar.

Frank untied his apron, carefully folded it, and handed it to the younger man. Frank's heavy jowls sagged and his forehead was furrowed with concern. "I don't think Marge is going to like this," he said. "It's the third time this month."

"Don't know how he does it," John observed, visibly relieved at having the drunken man out of the bar and out of his care. "Stays dry all week, bombs on Friday and Saturday."

"I don't think Marge is going to like this at all," Frank repeated, shaking his head.

"She should've married you, Frank. If she knew what was good for her."

"Cut it out."

"Cut what out?"

"Oh nothing." Frank went around to the other side of the car to get into the driver's seat.

"Listen. I gotta be getting back in there," John said, gesturing toward the open door of the lounge. "Don't want any customers getting upset."

"Sure," Frank said, slamming the car door shut beside him. The car was a large, older model Chrysler, but Frank filled it completely, at least the left front seat of it. The car dipped down on its springs beneath his weight. "Hey. Thanks for helping me get em in the car, John."

"No sweat, buddy. Any time." John stepped back as Frank drove away, the muffler of his car thrumming like the slow, deep barking of a Great Dane. John raised his hand as Frank pulled out onto the road, then he went into the lounge, closing the door behind him.

It was sometime between three and four in the afternoon when Frank pulled up onto the gravel driveway of the Mackey house. The house was in a small subdivision just east of town. None of the houses in this subdivision were large, almost all of them being one story clapboard structures with an attached single car garage. But they were generally well kept up. The cars parked in the driveways and along the streets in front of them were newer but less expensive models. Scattered among these was an occasional scratched, dented, working pickup truck, a few with lettering on the side, like Joe's Welding or Sam's Paint.

Considerable effort was required to get Lon out of the back seat. He was asleep and would not fully wake up. This meant he wasn't taking responsibility for his body weight and kept staggering this way and that, once he was out of the car, collapsing every few seconds on one leg or the other. Fortunately, Frank was a strong man. Putting his shoulder under one of Lon's arms and an arm around Lon's waist, he hauled him, like the sack of potatoes he'd become, still half asleep, up the sidewalk to the front door. Before they had quite reached it, Marge opened the door.

"Again?" Marge asked simply.

"Yes."

Their eyes met. There was a deep sadness in Frank's expression. He didn't like Marge seeing Lon this way.

"I know," Marge said abruptly, breaking off her gaze into Frank's eyes and shifting her glance to her husband. There was no anger or even disappointment in her expression, but there was a little moisture in her eyes. Even now that look, which she had exchanged with her former high school beau, had held, however impossibly, all the promise of what might have been.

"He'll be okay in a couple hours," Frank said. "Just needs to sleep it off." He entered the house and took Lon into his bedroom, laying him on top of the bedspread and taking off his shoes. Lon was immediately out cold, never having really woken up.

Leaving the bedroom and quietly shutting the door, Marge put her hand on Frank's shoulder, then kissed his cheek.

Frank flushed.

"Thank you," she said.

"Sure, Marge. You know how I am."

Marge dropped her hand from Frank's shoulder, running it caressingly along his sleeve. She gently squeezed his big arm and withdrew her hand. "We make decisions, Frank," she said. "Then we live with them."

"I know," Frank said.

Frank stood outside the front door for a moment after Marge had closed it. He didn't really feel like a man life had cheated. Lon was a good friend when he was sober. But, nevertheless, he had never felt it within his own power to find a wife.

An Old Woman

She was a simple old woman and she went shopping every day.

"The fresh fruit and vegetables will keep their strength," she would say. By which she no doubt meant they would retain their vitamins. "The fresh meat keeps its strength too," she would add. It was as if the yet uncooked flesh might, if knowledgeably prepared, communicate the animal's vigor directly to the shaping of a man's muscles, or the narrowing of a woman's waist, the childbearing strength of her uterus, and the firming of her breasts.

This old woman, who was Greek and lived in the Astoria section of New York, wore a plain black dress which terminated mid-calf above swollen ankles pressed into solid, black shoes. She bound her white hair tightly in a bun. She walked slowly, with an old woman's deliberation, from her apartment to the fruit and vegetable stand on Astoria Boulevard, then even more slowly with her load of daily provisions to the meat shop around the corner. Here, when in search of the smaller animals being sold, she sometimes obtained the whole carcass, dressed but not cut up. This she would, at the end of her morning shopping, take back to her kitchen (a work place equipped with simple but proper tools) and quarter or section the meat herself, according to need.

On her way back home along the boulevard, now on the north or opposite side of the street from the fruit stand, she purchased a fresh-baked round loaf of bread and a little of the strong goat cheese sold in that same dimly lit shop, the shelves of which were garnished with dusty jars of both home and factory canned vegetables and rows of condiments familiar to a Mediterranean palate.

Thelma Theotokas had a young, beautiful granddaughter named Anna, who generally addressed her as mama. Thelma lived alone with this girl; and, Anna, just turned seventeen, had her eyes on a young man, of whom Thelma did not approve. The young man was a second generation New Yorker, thoroughly Americanized, and had much of the free manners, easy ways of dress, and love of money of the new country with its hard, fast cities. On the other hand, Georgios—the owner of the fruit stand, an unmarried and eminently eligible bachelor in his late twenties who was of good family, quiet and circumspect—met with all of Thelma's expectations. He was, like Thelma, though much more recently, also a first generation arrival from a small coastal village on the island of Ios in the Aegean Sea. His childhood home was in fact only a short walk from Thelma's own ancestral birthplace.

"Why can you not see in Georgios any promise?" Thelma impatiently asked her granddaughter one Saturday morning as she gathered up her shopping basket and prepared to venture out into the glare of the morning sun and the motor-humming confusion of the street.

"He is too old, Mama. And his accent is thicker than goat cheese. Besides, I don't want to be the wife of a fruit seller. Or maybe even of a Greek. I'm an American."

"American shmerican," Thelma grunted as she went out into the street. "The young think they know everything in this country. And they know nothing at all. Nothing about life. A good husband is not for pleasure only. Pleasure alone is for dogs who have no cares. A good husband must be steady, responsible. It is disgraceful . . ."

"Good morning, Mama." It was Georgios speaking from behind his cash register, where he was waiting upon a customer. For Thelma had already arrived at the fruit stand, still muttering. Though no relation to her, of course, several of the most familiar shopkeepers called Thelma mama too.

"Ah, Georgios, you see I am in need of three fresh fat lemons. These are too small." Thelma squeezed a lemon into the palm of her hand, then released the helpless fruit into the wooden bin from which she had picked it up. It lay there bruised.

"I will find you what you need." Georgios stepped from behind his cash register inside the store, handing a sack of fruit and vegetables to the customer.

"Here," he said, out in the white, summer sunshine on the wide sidewalk. He dug into the back of the bin near the bottom, rolling the smaller lemons toward the front. "I will give you these three for the price of two." He smiled.

His teeth are not the best, but he is a good man, very steady and considerate, Thelma thought. "You are a good man, Georgios. That is just what I need."

On the way home Thelma reflected. Several street urchins, as she called them, ranging in age from seven to ten and not of good breeding, passed her on the sidewalk going the opposite direction. They were throwing a ball. One of them accidentally bumped into her. The boy did not stop to apologize but went on. Thelma turned, shaking her fist at the boy. "Mind your manners!" she said. "A boy like you should be at home doing his schoolwork."

The boy did not look back, nor did he look as if he spent much time at such things as homework assignments. He and his friends went on down the street.

At her apartment Thelma labored in the kitchen preparing a fine afternoon meal. Her brother and his forty-six year old son and wife were coming over. The middle-aged couple had no children.

In the bathroom Anna, now finally up for the day, pulled her very long dark hair back behind her shoulders and admired herself in the mirror. She had on denim shorts and a thin, yellow cotton shirt. The first three buttons of her shirt were undone and the shirt tails were pulled together and knotted above her midriff. She smiled wistfully, observing that her bellybutton looked sweet as sugar candy on her softly flattened belly. Then she untied the knot and tucked the shirt tails into her shorts. After this she buttoned two of the top buttons on her shirt and went out to tell her grandmother she would return in time for the family dinner.

Popular Forces

In the old French building some of the tiles were missing from the roof. In fact, half the roof was gone. Still, we used to sleep in there. Most of the time the hole in the roof didn't matter, and during the rainy season we would shelter ourselves as best we could under the tiles that remained. It was better than the bunkers.

This building was in the center of a small hamlet that lined a dirt road. Not much to look at but the road was considered important. So our nine man patrol was permanently assigned there to guard the village. We did supposedly have some help but it was hard to tell how much. A couple dozen Popular Forces soldiers were assigned to reinforce us. But we never saw all of them and few of them were reliable. During the day they were usually out on work projects for the District Chief.

Once, when we were hit at night by the VC, we had eight of them with us. They were strung out along the three bunkers we had facing the open field and distant tree line west of the village.

I was asleep when the shooting started. No mortars. Just rifle fire coming from the tree line. You have to be a good shot to hit anything at that distance—close to a thousand yards—but they were doing all right. You could hear some of the rounds thudding into the sandbags and the rest of them whistling faintly overhead. I had three of these Popular Forces guys with me. Two of them were on watch. The other one and I were asleep. It was our four hour rest break.

We were all on top of the bunker because it was the rainy season and the inside, which was dug part way into the ground, was always wet. We had an M-60 machine gun. The two guys on watch were having trouble getting the ammunition belt to feed into the gun and it kept jamming, so I got up, pulled the belt out, emptied the chamber, put the belt back in place and closed the cover. One of the soldiers started firing while I held the belt up and carefully fed it to the gun.

I don't think there is anything more beautiful than the way tracers arc at night, as long as they aren't coming toward you. They seem almost to float, to sail in a leisurely way toward their destination.

Once we got the machine gun going the firing stopped, the shooting that was coming from the tree line. Even though our other two bunkers were also answering their fire, the VC didn't stop until we opened up with the only machine gun. A thousand yards is really too far for sighting in with an M-16 rifle.

"They come back," the Popular Forces soldier said, releasing the trigger. He wiped his face with his sleeve. The other two soldiers were silent. I could feel as well as see their worry.

Maybe they will come back, maybe not, I thought. "Depends on how many are out there," I said.

"They come back," the soldier said.

Two Marines climbed onto the bunker. Steve and Roger. Roger, a sergeant, was our squad leader. They had been sleeping in the French building.

I don't know how the Viet Cong did it. It was maybe a half hour when all of a sudden we started catching fire from the village. The village! That was behind us and now they opened up at the tree line again. I started firing my M-16 at the tree line, lying as flat as I could. We had a small parapet of sandbags built up on that side but nothing on the other.

Men on the other two bunkers were firing in both directions. The PF I had helped with the machine gun was lying beside me, shooting carefully at muzzle flashes with his carbine.

Roger was swearing the way he always did when he was upset. He stood up and turned the machine gun around toward the village. Screaming at one of the other PFs, he got him to feed the belt to the gun. Steve was using his M-16, shooting toward the village. The VC had set fire to a couple of buildings. One of them was our French building. You could see human shapes moving about among the flames.

"God!" I said. There were several figures moving toward us out of the tree line. I saw them run zigzag into the field and hit the ground. I began to imagine one of the things I feared most: if we weren't all killed, we'd be captured.

That's when I noticed him. The other PF. I had turned to tell Roger what was happening and caught sight of him running. He veered at an angle, going toward the village but into the dark away from all the activity. I saw a couple more PFs running from the other bunkers.

"Don't let them get away!" Roger shouted. Steve shifted the barrel of his rifle to the right and fired. The PF spun half way around and fell to the ground. But he got back up, holding his arm, and stumbling into a run, kept on going.

"I should have told you to kill him," Roger said.

The machine gun had cleared the activity out of the village, so Roger turned it back toward the tree line. Steve crawled over to my left side. The PF helping Roger continued feeding the belt. I'm not sure what the other one was doing. I think he was watching the village.

It was hard to see in the dark by only the light of the tracers, but we thought we saw several figures run back into the tree line. Shortly after that the shooting stopped. Everything stopped.

In the morning we found our building a little charred but still usable. Some canteens, ammunition and a flack jacket were gone. But there weren't any bodies. I don't know about that damned PF or the others who ran off. We never saw any of them again.

The Bus and the Road Mine

You could hear the explosion for miles around. It was a big mine and when the bus hit it, that was the end of the bus. It was a local bus loaded with Vietnamese peasants going from one district market center to another. The Viet Cong must've meant that mine for one of our tanks or thick-hulled amphibious vehicles because the bus was shredded up like tin foil. You couldn't even make out what it was.

We were running a patrol nearby and had a radio and a corpsman with us, so we went over to check out the damage. We approached carefully because road mines are often followed by ambushes. When we got into the rice field next to the dirt road where the remains of the bus were, we started finding bodies and parts of bodies. All over the place. It was sickening. There were pigs and chickens scattered around too and some of them were alive. Then we discovered that some of the people were alive as well. Maybe half a dozen.

We found a woman lying in a twisted position on her back next to a paddy dike made of packed earth with grass growing on top. She still had all her limbs intact and had only minor cuts, but she was unable to move and just lay there looking up at the blue sky. The corpsman knelt beside her. He felt her in different places and tried very gently to straighten her body and make her comfortable.

"I don't think her back is broken," he said, "but I think just about every other bone in her body is."

He felt along one of the black silken legs of the woman's peasant pajamas while she watched him with a kind of apprehensive trust. She was a young, good looking Vietnamese. Vietnamese women are almost all beautiful when they're young. Before the beetle nut they chew ruins them by turning their mouths red and their teeth black, and before their faces get pock-marked from poor diet and sickness. It's the slender build, but with a figure, the small boned features and the long shiny black hair that do it.

"See," he said. He pulled her pant leg up to the knee. There were several black and blue spots along her shin and at one place about half way up the skin was broken and you could see a jagged piece of white bone. She winced when he barely touched her leg with his fingers.

Sgt. Sanchez came over. We were shin deep in paddy water and the woman was also lying in the water, but with her head propped against the paddy dike. "I had Baker radio for a helicopter," he said. "We found a couple more over there. They're in pretty bad shape."

"Like this one," the corpsman said.

The sergeant stood there contemplating her for a moment, then turned around and walked away, sloshing water in his jungle boots and crushing bunches of healthy green young rice plants into the mud under the water as he went.

When the chopper arrived our corpsman was dressing the wound on a little boy about five years old. He was found sitting alone out in the same rice field. He was sitting up in the water whimpering, looking at his right hand which was almost completely severed at the wrist, hanging by a tendon or two and a piece of skin. I don't know what gave him the presence of mind at that age, but he was holding his wrist tightly with the other hand, cutting off most of the flow of blood. It saved his life. Even then there was enough blood in the water all around him to make it appear as if there couldn't be any left in him. This boy had been blown the furthest out into the field of any of them. The few survivors must have been the ones riding on top of the bus with the chickens and pigs.

Just as the chopper touched down, pushing the paddy water away in waves with its prop wash, there was a thud, then a couple more, and a patter of several more bullets hit the water beside the helicopter.

We all went down into the water.

"Sniper, damn it! Johnson, get a couple people and go around that tree line. See if you can get in behind him." Everyone was returning fire and it was pretty clear there was only one VC out there from the way the rounds came in, one at a time with three hits on the helicopter's landing gear and a few extra in the water.

I took two members of my fire team and we worked our way around to the left at a low run through the paddy water. Hard going. He wasn't taking any more pot shots at us, but we didn't know if he'd taken off or was still lying in the tree line.

On the other side we caught sight of a young Vietnamese male, dressed like any other peasant, running as fast as he could along a dike away from us. All three of us fired almost simultaneously and he fell with a splash into the cold, early morning paddy water. Behind us the helicopter rose into the air, taking out the worst of the wounded Vietnamese.

Fire Base

It wasn't much of a firebase: a platoon of Marines and some howitzers. Ours were one five five millimeter guns but the Army had a one seven five there. If you were standing next to it when it was fired, the blast would knock you back a few feet. It could make for an unpleasant surprise if you weren't used to it.

The hill was an awful place. It was bad because we didn't have clear fields of fire. I don't mean we didn't cut most of the brush on its slopes. We did. But it grew back fast and the whole valley was jungle. That's why we were there: to observe VC traffic in the jungle. There was plenty of it but you couldn't see much. So we ran patrols in the area but they seemed to always know we were there. That probably had to do with the fact that there was a small hamlet nearby. The villagers there had a few miserable fields of things like rice and corn and they fished the river for shrimp with nets, but I don't really see how they got their living.

My point is this. After we held that hill through several hard firefights at night and took heavy casualties, they moved us away and abandoned it. We were even overrun one night but that's not when they moved us. It was a few weeks later.

The time I'm thinking of now was right after the night we were overrun. It was on one of our visits to the village. We didn't make many of them.

The choppers had come in the morning at first light to take out our wounded. But we still had our dead. Nobody had come yet from battalion headquarters with a truck to remove them. So we had the eight men killed in action, their bodies stacked like cordwood on the landing zone under army blankets with just their boots sticking out. A couple were killed by mortars, including one Army gun crewman. Almost all the other dead were from the part of our perimeter where the Viet Cong had broken through the wire. They had hit one of our bunkers with a rocket-propelled grenade.

The other one was John. He went out with the reaction patrol, which tried to flank the VC assault with some diverting fire. I think it did help to break them up and that cut off the support for the ones who had gotten inside our perimeter. But John took a round in the face. That's what Sgt. Jeffers told me but I didn't want to see it.

I was sick of that hill. So was everyone else. So was John, long before he got it. Whenever the sun comes up you always feel good. It's warm and you can see. There's always a sense of relief. You got through the night. But that only makes you feel guilty when a friend has just been killed.

We had to go into the village because—well, I'm not sure why we went into the village. Some guys from battalion headquarters showed up in a jeep with an interpreter and they needed a patrol for security. So four of us went along. There were three of them: a lieutenant and two enlisted, one of whom could speak Vietnamese. A little girl led us and we were very careful going down, keeping low and observing the brush. We let her get way out ahead of us. You couldn't see much and we didn't trust her. We didn't trust anybody in that hamlet.

She went out of sight around some brush and then there was an explosion. When we got to her she was lying there whimpering. There was blood on the grass and her left foot was gone about six inches above the ankle. You could see the splintered end of the shin bone, the torn muscle and blood pooling. I put a tourniquet on her. Then we carried her back up the hill and got battalion headquarters on the radio. That's where our company commander was. He sent us a chopper, which came from Division at Da Nang. It came over, barely touched down while I shoved the seven or eight year old girl into the arms of a crewman hanging out the door, then it went up again and became a dot in the blue sky.

We went back to the hamlet and the guys from battalion took care of their business, which now included telling the little girl's mother and an aunt, I think, that she was being flown to the civilian hospital in Da Nang. Then we climbed back up to the firebase.

What I keep remembering is that the little girl didn't scream or cry. She whimpered a bit; that was all. And we had been afraid to even trust her.

Black Pillars of Smoke

I'm not sure what civilian agency she represented. I think it was AID. She was young, fat, blond and either Dutch or German. She flew in one morning by helicopter to see the two thousand detainees we'd rounded up and enclosed in concertina wire. At the time she arrived we were feeding them plain boiled rice cooked in big black kettles over an open fire outdoors. In the near distance, across the Song Xuong River, were black pillars of smoke rising from the villages the detainees had come from.

The helicopter had suddenly and unexpectedly appeared out of the blue sky and set itself down near the large concertina wire enclosure. The young woman, about five feet four inches, weighing about one hundred and forty pounds, got out with a little help, looking clean and fresh as cut flowers. She got out and sank to her ankles in thick, partially dried mud. Her face showed no reaction but it didn't look relaxed. Our battalion Sergeant Major, a wiry, freckled, red headed Marine with a face dried out and lined by weather, cigarettes and hard liquor, led her over to the enclosure.

"These are the detainees brought in from the villages in the Viet Cong controlled area across the Song Xuong," he said.

"Yes, I know. How long have they been here?"

"Some for two days, some one, some still being brought in."

"Any sick?"

"Malaria, tuberculosis, dysentery . . ."

"Awful." She was looking now over the treetops toward the black columns of smoke. The ground shook occasionally with the sound of bombs, and American jets could be seen diving down and rising back up into the clear sky. It was a bright sunny day except for the black smoke.

The Sergeant Major got a glint in his eye. "Beautiful day," he said.

"Awful!"

A group of the detainees, some old men and a number of women and children, were squatting on the ground eating balls of rice with their fingers off paper plates we'd supplied them. They were squatting on their heels and could sit for amazingly long periods of time like that. All were silent and had blank faces with the stares of those who've lost everything.

The AID woman finally looked away from the burning villages. "We have facilities for most of them at the Nguoi Viet compound in Da Nang. What have you done with the worst cases?"

"They were medevacked out by chopper to the civilian hospital in Da Nang this morning."

"And these are being fed rice?"

"Yes."

"A strict diet of rice?"

"Yes."

"Awful."

"That's what they eat. We haven't been getting any complaints. Would you like to speak to any of them?"

"No!" Her response was almost a recoil.

The Sergeant Major smiled. "Out here you get used to the conditions." He looked at her feet, the chubby white ankles spattered with mud.

There was a sudden commotion of rumbling and creaking. A tank appeared in a cloud of yellow dust and roared past us at thirty miles an hour, then continued on down the hard packed dirt village road, which was already dry after the recent rain. The top of the tank, an M-48 with a 90 millimeter gun, was covered with infantrymen.

"They're certainly in a hurry," the woman remarked.

"Firefight in the next hamlet down the road there." Now that he mentioned it, you could hear the sporadic small arms fire.

"More prisoners, I suppose."

"More bodies. Maybe some of them ours."

"Awful."

The Sergeant Major contemplated her for a moment as one would a stray dog eating something unsavory.

"I will make my report," she said. In the background was the high pitched whine of the helicopter as its rotors slowly began to turn. She turned around and started to trudge toward it. A crewman hopped out and helped her aboard. The Sergeant Major remained standing beside the concertina enclosure. He took out a cigarette and lit it. The helicopter lifted off with her in it, rose into the sky and went away.

An American two and a half ton truck pulled up. Several Marines hopped down from the open rear end of it and began pulling large burlap bags full of rice off it. They dropped one and it burst, the clean white grains pouring over one another out onto the ground. The ground was dry and dusty here near the road. The only mud was in the area around the enclosure, which seemed to hold moisture after a rain longer than anyplace else.

As soon as the bag hit the ground, local village women came out of nowhere, scrambling on hands and knees in the dirt, fighting over the grains, bickering, weeping and shouting, scooping both dirt and grains into their conical hats and the folds of their blouses. The Marines stood and watched.

The Portrait

The isolation had come by slow degrees. He had dropped out of art school. He had quarreled with his friends. He never married. Gradually losing confidence in himself, he began to drink. Nevertheless, he continued to paint.

At age thirty-five David Mankiewitz had almost ceased to care. He was able to make a living because he'd learned to give the world what it wanted. He gave it nothing of himself.

Then he met Sally Cartwright, a part-time feature article writer and reporter for a local Seattle arts magazine.

* * *

After having heard of him through a friend, Sally had gone about the city to see his work. It was of a semi-abstract nature: simple figures in local settings, easy to understand. The kind of paintings every bank has a wall for. She thought them trite. But there was something in them. Though she couldn't have said what, it intrigued her.

An aficionado of Spanish painting, she particularly loved Zurbaran and Ribera for their spiritual realism. Then there was Goya. How was it that Goya, like the Frenchman Degas after him, could spiritualize paint, could make color float ethereally in the membraneless ether of an observing mind?

But such musings told her nothing about David. Everything she'd seen of his had been unpromising. Yet . . . She made the call.

* * *

He arranged to meet her in a small cafe in the university district. It was a Tuesday, an overcoat day in spring. No rain. Just an overcast sky. It was one in the afternoon and, when she came through the door, he was sitting where he'd said he would be. He didn't recognize her at first. His thoughts were on the question of why she would want to interview him. He knew she'd seen only his commercial work, and he had no illusions about the quality of it.

Though not thinking her to be the reporter he was waiting for, he was nevertheless absentmindedly looking in her direction when she swung the glass door open. She was pretty in a way. He might've described her as softly attractive. Fairly tall, her build was somewhat stocky, her hair falling in gentle, crepelike curls, flowing, shoulder length, somewhere between brown and gold. Her face was small, oval, pleasantly lacking in sharp features. It lit up with a smile when she saw him.

She came briskly over to his table, putting out her hand, which he took. He noticed her left hand had no wedding ring on it. "May I join you?" she asked.

"It's okay with me," he said in a noncommittal tone of voice. He wasn't trying to be impolite and certainly not enthusiastic either. Neutral tones were best worn for such occasions. But an unexpected warmth engulfed him as she sat down. He began to feel animated. He looked at her more closely. "I'm David Mankiewitz," he said. It occurred to him that it should seem rather odd she hadn't introduced herself or asked his name.

They talked for awhile. She took notes. He had ordered coffee and a doughnut for himself. She now did the same. She asked a few questions about his art, then delved into his background. He was uncomfortable but didn't know how to divert her. In fact, he felt powerless. It was as though he'd been drugged.

She sensed his discomfort at the probing, but was curious. There was something here worth going after.

"David," she said finally, "I think there's work you haven't been showing."

"What do you mean?"

"I mean I think you're a better painter than what I've gathered from what I've seen."

Up to this point he had responded to her questioning as though he were interviewing with a bank officer for a loan. The conversation had been businesslike and impersonal. Now they looked at each other in silence.

Her eyes were gray. They smiled and were the source of that warmth he'd been feeling. He was stunned to realize she had matter-of-factly dismissed the quality of his public work. But it didn't cause him much concern.

"Well, I've done a few things I don't show," he said.

"Can I see them?"

He thought of the squalid mess his house was in. He was using his living room for a studio. It had good lighting to the north and west.

His mind drifted. Of course, the lighting was quite uniform on overcast days like this. It gave everything a silver hue. Somewhat depressing if you weren't used to it.

"Well, let's go," he said abruptly.

They got up and left the cafe.

He had an old car of the kind one drives in preference to riding a bus. The buses took forever to get anywhere. The car bore the risk of not getting there at all. They parked it at the base of a hill and climbed a long flight of concrete steps.

His home in West Seattle was the northern half of a two-story, side-by-side duplex that faced west over the slate gray waters of Puget Sound. Being something of a gardener by shifts of mood, he was proud of its outward appearance, for he had cultivated climbing vines and brambles, which were loaded with the red, yellow and purple blossoms of rose and clematis. Gulls were about, in the air and on the ground.

Sally took a deep breath and let it out. "It smells of the sea," she said, stating the obvious.

"I should hope so!" he responded laughing. He opened the front door. "Careful you don't stumble over the cat."

Sally looked at her feet before stepping inside the doorway. There was nothing there. She did notice something yellow, tiger-striped lying on the inside sill of a bay window. It hopped down and meowed as they came in, rubbing itself against David's pant leg.

"I imported him from India," he said.

Sally smiled and raised her eyebrows. "I see he's of the Bengal variety," she remarked.

"Well, he's small. It's the cat food. No goat or young gazelle in the can."

"Oh, do tigers eat gazelles?"

"Depends on the local supermarket," he said.

"Yes, of course." She smiled. How far were they going to go with this? By this time she had taken a thorough survey of the studio. It was a mess. Rags and brushes everywhere, some of the brushes left uncleaned with the paint dried stone hard upon them. There was an acrid, suffocating odor of that paint, a hint of turpentine, and a general atmosphere of stale air. Half a dozen easels were tossed about, two of them folded and leaning against a wall, the others lying on the floor. There were no completed canvases anywhere. She looked enquiringly at David.

"Upstairs," he said. "Let me take your sweater and get you something out of the kitchen." He hung the sweater in a closet, then struggled with the bay window. It was a large wooden type that was hoisted upward by ropes on pulleys built inside its frame. It wouldn't budge. "Painted shut," he said, giving up. "I should've tried it before."

Brother! she thought. He's never opened the window before?

After he had settled her on an uncomfortable, wooden, straight-backed chair—one of several scattered randomly about the room, where not all of them were standing up—he went into the kitchen. He returned with a clear glass filled with a transparent liquid resembling tea. Then he climbed upstairs to retrieve some paintings.

While he was gone, Sally began to seriously question her motives. "Why am I here?" she whispered aloud to herself. "This guy lives like a rat in a drainage tunnel."

He came downstairs with two canvases, one suspended from each hand. This manner of carrying them made them look heavy, like cutting boards he might've stored in his bedroom closet. He put them against a wall, then grabbed two easels and dragged them over in front of her. She was still seated and feeling now not a little embarrassed.

"There," he said, putting the easels up and setting a canvas on each of them. "What do you think?" When she didn't answer, he added, "I know they're not as good as you'd hoped."

"No," she said, unable to form her thoughts. "They're good."

"Good, huh." He sat down on another straight-backed chair. "I can accept that."

"No, really good," she said. "Let me think about it, will you." There was impatience in her voice.

Built tall and slender, David was not a hairy man, but he did have a thin, scraggly beard. He ran his hand through it while he waited.

There was something in the two paintings which was similar to the ones that were hanging all about the city. But these were not bank paintings. In these David's palette was cool, the composition restrained. Their semi-abstract forms suggested not only figures but an artful use of line, the whole being held together by subtle modulations of color and light.

No, that isn't what I'm seeing, Sally thought. There's a depth too. It's as if these figures have emerged from a smoky, indefinable background.

She looked at David. Could this fragile man have done this? She was about to say something when she dropped her glass, shattering it on the bare wooden floor. "Oh, I'm terribly sorry," she apologized, getting up out of the chair.

David picked up several paint rags and began soaking up the liquid and gathering glass. Other than the tinkle of the shards, which he was moving into a pile, there was silence in the room. The cat was back on its window sill, grinding its teeth. A gull was passing before the window, craning its neck to get a look. It seemed almost to jeer.

The mess cleaned up, Sally offered a few inane comments, standing in the kitchen doorway while David put the broken glass in a garbage can under the sink. He closed the cabinet door with a bang that startled her.

"I . . . I can't seem to get across what I'm trying to say, David," she said awkwardly. "Let me go back to work and put my thoughts together."

"All right," he said.

They returned to the university district, which was where the tiny editorial office for the arts magazine was located. She got out of the car, waved a quick good-by and went into the building.

Okay, he said to himself, sitting in the car and adjusting to the situation. He drove home. There he sat in his studio and looked out at the sea gulls.

* * *

Sally did not remain in the magazine office but went home, which was a few blocks off University Avenue. She worked part-time at the magazine and was a full-time graduate student at the University. Her academic concentration not being art history but the history of Western civilization in general, she was hoping to receive her doctorate within three years, which she knew to be an ambitious goal, considering her busy schedule. But she was not one to dally in her efforts.

Her apartment was somewhat like David's in that it had been a duplex. But the resemblance ended there. The duplex had been further subdivided into four separate units, a pair of covered, outdoor, wooden staircases approaching the two upper story dwellings from opposite sides of the building. She lived in the one that faced toward Lake Union, which lay too far south in a sea of urban concrete to be seen from her windows. The apartment was also occupied by another woman. They were both graduate students in their mid to late twenties.

Mimi, her roommate, came home shortly after she did, returning from a class. This woman's most distinctive characteristics were that she was small, blond and pretty. Generally wearing shorts to class in summer, she wore very short skirts everywhere else in every kind of weather. Flirtatious with men, she was talkative in public, and this worldly, animated chatter was invariably devoid of any sort of intellectual interest.

At home with Sally was another matter. For Mimi was a brilliant scholar, one of Sally's classmates.

After she had tossed her backpack into the bedroom, allowing it to find temporary lodging wherever the laws of aerodynamics and appropriate forces should direct it, she asked Sally how her interview had gone.

"Not so well, I think," Sally said.

"What do you mean, not so well?" Mimi asked. As she spoke she went into the kitchen and got a soft drink out of the refrigerator. She popped the top, came into the living room, and sat down, crossing her legs. Sally envied those shapely legs. Mimi was wearing a short skirt.

"He's kind of strange."

"You mean his work isn't very good. I've seen some of his stuff around town."

"No, some of it's surprisingly good." Sally paused. "He lives like a slob."

Mimi laughed. "Haven't you ever met an artist before?" she asked.

"I've read . . ."

"No, no. I mean today in real life."

"Does he have to look and act like a hippie to do good work?"

"No. But some of them do. It's . . . it's bohemian." Mimi grinned. She seemed perfectly at ease with the idea that genius and wretchedness could be bound up together in the same human package. Sally wasn't. It was incongruous to her that what she considered to be the best of mankind should look and behave like the worst.

"I don't get it," she said simply. She smiled. Mimi's gaiety was infectious.

"Get what?" Mimi asked. "When someone makes as little as most artists do, he tries to compensate by pretending it doesn't matter."

"Not this guy. He lives better than we do. He just isn't clean and orderly about it."

"Well, go interview an engineer or a banker then."

"Oh get real! What do I know about science or business?" They were both laughing now, and the levity lifted Sally's spirits.

"We didn't finish the interview," she said. "I've got to see him again."

"Oh?" There was a twinkle in Mimi's eyes. When it came to men, her imagination only ran in one direction.

"No, not that."

"Then what?"

"His work. It really is good. Mystical, I think. Oh, but how can such a man be mystical?"

"Some of the quietest men I know are terrors in the bedroom."

"Will you get off that, Mimi? The problem is he's a terror with an apparently quiet mind."

"Does he drink or do drugs?"

"I don't know. I've heard he drinks."

"Well, there you have it. He's under the influence of a mind-altering substance."

"Meaning what?"

"Meaning he lives in two worlds. Which is the sober one? That's the question."

Both women were laughing themselves to tears now, and the conversation had become so outrageous as to render itself meaningless.

Over the next few days, Sally decided it would be a good idea to write her article without a second interview. She knew enough from what she'd seen to say something constructive, and she felt she didn't have time for the lengthy investigation required for a major feature article. She'd already lost an afternoon she couldn't afford. She had papers to complete for the spring quarter, not to mention work on her thesis. The quarter page article she submitted to the newspaper-format, art magazine she worked for appeared on the next to last page.

In the weeks that followed she began to feel guilty. David had never called her or the magazine, and she had certainly dropped him. What must he think? Probably nothing, she would assure herself. A disorderly house is the expression of a disorderly mind. Still, her own mind, or heart, persisted in bringing the matter up at the oddest moments.

The point was that she had indicated there would be a second interview. Was it honest or fair never to say a word further about it? And then the article itself—so short and buried in the magazine— was something of an insult. What must he think?

"I don't care!" she shouted in exasperation one afternoon alone in her apartment.

That evening she and Mimi were having dinner at a small restaurant on University Avenue. While eating, she had brought up the problem of recurring guilt. Of course, she had mentioned it lightly between mouthfuls of food. Mimi seemed to shrug it off as too minor a thing to be concerned about. But then halfway through the meal she suddenly burst out with, "Why don't you invite David up to the apartment?"

"What? Are you crazy? What on earth for?"

"Listen. I'm serious, Sally. I've been thinking about it. You like this guy, in spite of all you say. I can see that."

"Well, I feel I've been a little unfair."

"More than that. I'm telling you no one worries about offending someone they don't care about. Not for weeks on end."

"You do if you have principles you feel you've violated. This guy has real ability as an artist, but I don't think his sense of self-worth is very good. God knows what I've done to that."

Mimi studied her friend for a moment. Then she said slowly, "Okay, maybe you're not in love with him. But it bothers you. Tell him you're as surprised as he is that your article was cut short."

"I'd rather not tell him any more lies."

"Well, tell him whatever you want. If you don't want to be alone, we'll both lift his spirits." Mimi put her hand on Sally's forearm. "Listen, honey, I know this has been driving you nuts. One night of treating him like royalty ought to repair any damages done."

"All right. Well. But what do I say?"

"Just apologize for the short article and leave it at that. Then invite him over. If he says yes, well and good. If he says no, you've done your best. You can use your busy schedule as an excuse for not having interviewed him again, and you can say this is your attempt to make things right in a relaxing way."

* * *

Sally called David and was unable to get hold of him the first few times. When she did, she thought he sounded a little despondent. Or is he just drunk? she thought upon hanging up the phone. But she pushed the idea out of her mind. She wasn't going to be unfair.

David arrived at the apartment at six in the evening. A little early. He was supposed to get there by six-thirty. Mimi was in the kitchen preparing the meal. She was dressed in a short, bright, large patterned dress: a rose, lemon, leaf green and royal blue, Hawaiian muumuu with an eight inch slit in the side. Sally was wearing blue jeans and a simple cotton top. David was also in shirt and jeans. But he startled Sally when she opened the door. His beard was gone.

"You're clean as a whistle," she said. The words had escaped her, and she immediately blushed.

"Oh yeah, I cut if off a while back," he said touching his face. "I was feeling kind of down and needed a change."

"Oh," Sally said. She hoped she hadn't been the cause of his feeling down. "Come on in."

She got him a beer, serving it in the can. Then Mimi came out of the kitchen. David immediately noted how attractive she was but decided that wasn't what he was there for.

"I hope you like tossed greens and teriyaki steak," she said.

"Sounds good."

"Well, it would be too late if it didn't."

They both laughed. Sally felt a little embarrassed and uncomfortable. She was well aware of her roommate's infectious personality and attractive looks.

But the evening went well. Mimi even chose to display her full range of intelligence in the presence of a man. They discussed a good many things, and she was able to draw David out on what he hoped, or had once hoped, to do with his art.

Sally listened to this discussion, adding few comments of her own. But she found herself deeply moved. Much of what she had seen but resolutely failed to fully acknowledge in the two paintings David had shown her was now being revealed in his very manner and explanation. Here, in fact, was a truly serious artist, a man who had never quite given up, in spite of his best efforts to do so.

David went home about ten o'clock. Sally and Mimi decided he had been a model guest.

"Well, what do you think?" Sally asked, when they'd settled back into the living room.

"Think about what?" Mimi responded in a manner resembling a yawn. Still dressed in her short muumuu, she was sprawled comfortably in an armchair with one leg carelessly looped over the arm, looking as if she might be about to go to sleep.

"David. What else? David as a person, an artist."

"He's okay," Mimi said indifferently. An unstrapped sandal was hanging loosely from the foot that was suspended in the air.

"Oh, come on! What was all that talk about art for? I didn't know you knew so much about it."

"Listen," Mimi said, looking solemnly at her friend, then smiling, "I think there's a lot there. You ought to take him seriously. If you don't, I might."

"What? You're going to . . ."

"Take it easy, honey. I'm just kidding. In a way. What I mean is that if you don't want him I might be interested. He isn't bad looking, you know. And he's bright. He doesn't seem to mind a woman who talks intelligently either."

"A lot of men wouldn't, if you'd let them know."

"Hey, I know men, baby. Okay?"

"Well, you know more than I do."

Mimi got up, adjusting her sandal, and went to take a shower. She pulled her muumuu up over her head and dropped it outside the bathroom door. She left her sandals out there too, laying her undergarments on the toilet seat. She came out of the shower carrying, first the undergarments, then her dress and sandals into the bedroom, her body wrapped in an oversized pink bath towel. Then she found Sally in the kitchen washing dishes.

"I needed that," Mimi said. "Cooking makes me feel hot and greasy." She took a beer out of the refrigerator. "This stuff just makes me feel hot," she remarked, popping the tab and drinking from the can. Her blond hair was darkened from being wet and was bound up on her head in a smaller towel. Both women laughed at the double entendre in the word hot.

Sally wondered how anyone who never seemed to think about anything but men and sex could be so bright. Loftiness of intellect and earthiness of imagination were not well matched attributes in her own moral handbook. Looseness of behavior, in her opinion, was an even less well matched companion to a highly-wrought mind. But then, what was high-mindedness anyway? She wasn't sure she knew herself. She just knew she wanted to attain it if she could. She went a little too far sometimes, she supposed.

Before going to bed, the two women got into a conversation again about David's art. With the beer—and several others before it—in her system, Mimi was feeling even more loquacious than usual. But the alcohol high did not dull the keenness of her perceptions. As she spoke, she had only to remove the towels and put on her nightgown to fling herself deliciously into bed, wetting the pillow with her damp hair. The sheets were cool, and she felt it a good place to anchor the slight spinning of her head. For she did not hold alcohol well.

"It's true I've never seen his painting," she said. "His serious work anyway. But from what you've told me it fits. There's something otherworldly about that guy, the way he talks. You know, maybe he lives the way he does because it just doesn't really matter."

"What do you mean?"

"Well, I mean if he has his head in the clouds—you'll pardon my putting it that way. If his mind isn't on worldly things so much, maybe he just doesn't notice the mess. What seems disorderly to some might not be to others."

Lying in the dark in her bed, Sally thought about that for awhile. In the silence of the room, she could hear her roommate's breathing soften as she dropped off into sleep.

She had to concede that what Mimi had said made sense. But the disorderliness she had observed extended far beyond a messy studio. The man was irregular and seemed irresponsible in his person. She'd heard things. Oh, if she could only be a little less easily influenced by hearsay and opinions! But at least some of it was true. She could see that.

She began to brood upon herself. Certainly she could also see she was a prude. She would no doubt die a lonely virgin, tight as a leather thimble, she thought crudely, wanting in her self-pity to be cruel to herself. Well, she didn't really care. She couldn't be a woman without principles.

Then she began to feel guilty about the implied harsh judgment she had just passed upon her friend in applying the possession of principles only to herself. Mimi is so sweet, she confessed. Incomprehensible, but sweet. No one better ever hurt her. It would be a crime against God, no matter what she does.

During these interminable moments of increasingly lugubrious thought on the part of Sally, Mimi began to snore. Sally got up quietly, went over to her roommate's bed, and gently shook her shoulder. Mimi rolled over in her sleep and stopped snoring.

In the morning both women had to attend class, so they left together to have breakfast in the cafe where Sally had met David. They even sat at the exact table where she had met him. So, whenever the door to the place opened to admit another customer, she found herself glancing up as if she expected him to come through it.

"This is ridiculous," she mumbled, drinking her coffee.

"What is?" Mimi asked.

"Oh, nothing."

"Come on. Mama knows her little girl," Mimi cooed loudly, laughing.

"Little girl! It would take one and a half of you to make one of me."

"Mama hatches a big one."

"Hey. What's with you girls? You want to let us in on the joke?" A young man in a party of three at the table behind Sally was turned around facing them. He was a classmate of theirs. He had been out with Mimi a couple times and felt, perhaps undeservedly, the privilege of familiarity.

"Nothing *you'd* know what to do with," Mimi responded with a big grin.

The young man took this pill with calm resignation and turned around to face his companions, who didn't know the two women.

The women finished their light breakfast in animated conversation made somewhat self-conscious by the unwanted attention. Then they left together, one immediately for class, the other to the library to wait out the hour remaining before hers.

* * *

The problem, David thought, is that this woman can't make up her mind to leave me alone. She's like a kitchen sink with hot and cold water coming out of the same spigot. Well, he'd enjoyed himself. Mimi was a good cook. And what a gorgeous woman she was!

He wondered if anyone had ever been inside Sally's dress. Probably not, he decided. Then he began to feel unjustified in having had such a thought. But what was it about her that commanded this moral response?

He was an enigma in his own eyes. There were times when the mystery was himself. It got into his art. His best work. He was, after all, quite an expert at turning out trash. To feed himself he had to feed others what they were capable of ingesting.

Prostituting himself in this way had made him a self-hater. That had introduced an element of crudeness into him. For he felt a good deal of self-contempt at times and consequently despised the world for it.

Having just come home from the dinner at Sally's apartment, he was now sitting in his studio, looking at the two canvases he had shown her almost a month before. He had carelessly left them in their place all these weeks. A can of beer was in his hand. It wouldn't be the last one he would drink before he went to bed. He could hold several six-packs when called upon to do so. As a matter of fact, he performed this task easily and often.

He was presently sitting in a totally darkened house, using a flashlight to peer at each canvas in turn, as though he were a viper examining mice with its heat-sensitive pits. He had told Mimi he was trying to get at the ground of his own being. Now, what did that mean? One said anything to justify oneself under interrogation, he decided. After the third or fourth beer he went upstairs with a six-pack.

In the morning he had a hangover. It was Saturday. Normally he worked on Saturdays, but not this one. He had stayed up too late. He could see it was a clear day, because light was pouring in from behind the window blind on one side, and that's what the birds were telling him, as well. They, robins mostly, were outrageously beautiful in their singing. They sounded like a clear running brook in a green meadow. They suggested warm summer heat and a cool breeze under the shade of trees. I've got to get up, he said to himself. But he rolled over and slept until noon.

When he finally did get out of the house, he went into town and caught a ferry over to Bainbridge Island. The smell of water, grass and forest was in his nostrils. Puget Sound was blue under a sunny sky, and the island was green like a jewel. He bought a newspaper and ate in a small cafe beside the water.

There were two young boys out on the dark mud tidal flat in front of the cafe balcony. Their pants rolled up to the knees, they were barefoot, and their footprints ran out in parallel rows in all directions, showing where they'd been. One was carrying a bucket and both had hand trowels. They were clamming. The ocean smell of Puget Sound had gone out with the tide, and what remained behind was an odor of salt and decaying seaweed which was strewn about in thick, wet bundles and long, dripping strands, where it had been left behind by the receding water. Beyond the boys, near the softly lapping, dirty foam edge of that water, were shore birds, darting about on their stilt legs, punctuating the wet sand with long slender bills.

Sally came into his mind again. She had never really left it. Of course, there were moments when he also contemplated the pure sensual delight of Mimi in her short dress. She was so lively and shapely. Quick in the head too. What a woman! But Sally always returned to his thoughts. The mystery of her, and something else, kept him wondering.

He looked up. The two boys were running across the tidal flat laughing. The shore birds took off in a long wheeling arc, circling the wall of forest that enclosed the inlet. The boy carrying the bucket of clams dropped it, spilling some of its contents, then picked it up without noticing the loss. Just as he did, a great blue heron uttered a gronk and lumbered into the sky. He dropped the bucket again. Cupping their hands over their eyes to block the sun, both boys stopped and watched the big bird sail up over the trees. The heron disappeared. Disappointed, they turned back to their clamming.

But soon one of them found something more interesting. Near the water's edge there were hundreds of crabs. They had been part of the natural bounty the shore birds were feeding on. The boys began gathering them with delight.

David smiled. If the clamming was supposed to supply a family dinner, these boys' harvest was going to be a great disappointment.

Later, during his return trip to Seattle on the ferry, as he watched the city skyline grow into view, his mind wandered. The ferry slowed before docking, the chugging of its engines, smell of oily water and cry of seagulls announcing its approach.

Suddenly he felt himself seized with a desire to get to work. The afternoon light was turning hazy, but that wouldn't matter. He had the bustle of Elliott Bay and the roaring city in his veins. All about him lay a fullness, activity, an earnestness of life.

He took a bus home, since he hadn't brought his car downtown. While passing over the bridge to West Seattle, he looked at the tall, orange, metal cranes in the bay: big mantis legs of steel which were used to load and unload barges and ships. They were the hooks and jaws of this city, taking in much of its nourishment and regurgitating its wealth.

At home he set up an easel, put a fresh canvas on it, and began to paint. He did not work from preliminary sketches. Nor did he look out his windows.

He was indifferent to everything but the impulse within him. Thus he laid on pigments thickly and unmixed with a brush. In the background to this portrait—for it was a portrait from imagination—he used a pallet knife, plastering on shades of gray and cobalt blue in broad, heavy strokes that left the paint ridged between applications of the knife. The effect was like a rough concrete wall standing dimensionless behind the figure.

The image was clearly recognizable as that of Sally, though sharper in its features. It bore a brooding inward look, and, though modeled in perspective, seemed to recede into its background. It was elusive, appearing to pull itself away from the visual grasp and mental comprehension of the viewer, as though it were the exposed, embarrassed image of a soul.

He worked rapidly. Within a few hours—during which time he did not move from in front of the canvas—it was over. Laying his paint-smeared palette, knife and brushes aside, he stepped back self-consciously to have a look. It repelled him. God, it's brutal, he thought. I'll have to figure out what it means sometime. He shrugged. What the hell. He didn't think he really cared about it now that it was finished.

That night he was drinking alone in a bar he often frequented in downtown Seattle, when to his astonishment he recognized someone at a nearby table. When he turned to get a better look, her eyes met his. It was Mimi, who was out with someone he'd never seen before. He quickly glanced away.

What's she doing here? he thought. It was a ridiculous question. Why shouldn't she be there? It was a public place.

"Oh no you don't!" he heard her voice call out. When he looked around again, she was advancing toward his table with laughter upon her mouth and in her eyes. Her teeth were perfect little pearls, and her parted lips had a quality of sensuousness he felt throughout his body. "You can't do that," she reiterated as she came up to him. "Just sit here and drink all by yourself."

"Why not?" he asked, smiling with self-conscious embarrassment. He was at a loss for words, and he could see the expression on the face of the other person at her table. It was one of surprise and bewilderment.

She pulled out a chair and sat down at his table. "Because I won't let you," she said. She'd obviously had too much to drink.

"What about *him*?" He glanced in the direction of the other table.

"Chuck, come on over here," she called. "I want you to meet an old friend."

"Old friend?" David wondered. He was physically uncomfortable. The room around him seemed to glow with light when he looked at Mimi.

The date joined them. He seemed a decent enough sort, willing to put up with such surprises. He pulled a chair over from an unoccupied table, since each table had only two. Before sitting down he shook David's hand.

Over the course of an hour and a half, the three of them lightly discussed a range of forgettable topics, such as where they'd been born and raised, what their favorite drink was, etc. Through it all Mimi's voice was bright and cheerful. She did not once mention Sally.

After this long interval of chatter, Chuck suggested politely that it might be time for him and Mimi to leave. She responded curtly that he could go if he wanted to. She was staying. Embarrassed and offended, he got up and left.

"Good," she said after he had gone. "I wanted to tell you something about Sally."

"What?" David asked.

"I think . . ." She started to laugh. "I'm sorry. I think she's in love with you. But she doesn't know it."

"She could've fooled me," he said.

Mimi frowned. "I know," she said. "I think she's a bit of a prude sometimes."

"But not you."

"No, not me." She smiled. "I wish I was. I don't know why I'm the way I am."

He put his hand on her arm. "I like you the way you are."

She looked at him in surprise, but she didn't withdraw her arm. "We shouldn't," she said with forthright penetration.

"Who is there to tell us we shouldn't?"

"I don't know. Sally?"

"What's she got to do with it?"

"She's my friend."

"Your friend tells you how to live?"

"I told you, I think . . ."

"And I told you she could've easily fooled me by the way she acts."

* * *

They went to David's house together. Entering in the dark, they went upstairs. In the morning when they came down, Mimi saw the portrait. "What's this?" she asked.

"Oh nothing. Something I did yesterday."

"Oh, Dave," she said, "we shouldn't have done it." She began to cry.

He tried to divert her, but her remorse was real and complete. She left his house in the same state of emotion, saying she would catch the bus. He was stunned. Her departure was as abrupt as their coming together had been.

After she had gone, he stood silently in the studio for several minutes. He felt uncomfortable but wasn't about to share in her sense of guilt. It's ridiculous, he thought. He went over and looked at the portrait. "See what you've done?" he said. "What is it with you anyway?"

Several weeks passed. He did not see either Mimi or Sally during this time. Of course, there was no reason he should. His path didn't, as a matter of routine, cross theirs. Still, he wondered at Mimi's sudden access of guilt. It seemed excessive to him. He studiously avoided looking at the portrait in the studio.

One evening, perhaps a week after her encounter with David, Mimi indirectly confessed her guilt to Sally. She told her she'd gone out with him. But she did not have the courage to admit she'd gone home with him.

Nevertheless, Sally guessed the unspoken part of the story. She didn't have to press for details. She knew her roommate well and saw it in her uncomfortable manner.

Though she insisted to herself that she had no claims and it was really none of her business, her manner toward Mimi grew formal and cold. Mimi alternately roasted and froze under this treatment. She chided herself for her loose morals. Nothing would relieve her of the sense of having betrayed her friend.

This went on for about two weeks. Then Sally developed a bold, or perhaps desperate, strategy. She couldn't help expressing the coldness she now felt toward Mimi, but she didn't want to destroy her friendship with her over something as tenuous as her own supposed interest in David.

She thought of it as a supposed interest because she'd never really admitted to herself that she'd had such feelings. This in spite of the fact that her present emotional turmoil made such an interest clear.

Her strategy was simple. David really was a good artist. That was beyond any doubt. So she would foster his serious work with another interview and article. It would be done in the interest of culture, not herself. Then, having emotionally survived such a harrowing episode, she could set her hurt feelings aside and resume her old friendship with Mimi.

When she called David, he was curt and not very responsive on the phone. But she did get an appointment to visit him at his home the following afternoon.

He spent the intervening time occasionally wondering why he had set up such an appointment. Vanity, I suppose, he thought. She says she wants to do another article on me. She's already seen my work. Well, what the hell. What can it hurt?

When Sally arrived by taxi and bus (she'd taken a taxi from the university district to catch the West Seattle bus downtown), he'd already had several beers, perhaps half a dozen. He was in the worst possible condition for receiving her. For he could be unpleasantly lax in manners when he was simultaneously drinking and dealing with someone toward whom he had mixed feelings.

"Come on in," he said, opening the door at the sound of the bell and giving a broad, low sweep of welcome with his free arm. His voice was oily with drink.

Sally stepped primly inside, advancing with small, hesitant steps like a schoolgirl. She surveyed him as one might a sausage tossed upon the soiled surface of a bar.

"Don't mind me. I'm a little relaxed today."

"I can see that," she answered icily.

He looked at her. Her response had splashed cold water upon his face. "I'm sorry," he said.

"For what?"

"Nothing. Would you like something to drink?"

"No!" Then her expression softened. There was that look in her eyes he'd noticed in the cafe. Her eyes always made him feel warm.

"You know," he said leading her into the studio, "I've already told you everything there is to say about my ideas on art. You and Mimi." He saw a flicker of discomfort on her face. She knows what happened, he thought. What the hell.

"I do have something to show you," he added, covering his own growing discomfort. He stopped in front of the portrait.

Sally's first reaction, following immediately upon recognition of herself in the image, was shock. Shock at the harsh angular manner of the conception. Offense too at the cold, alienating background.

Then she saw it differently. She understood something of the anger with which it had been painted. A suppressed anger, no doubt. But plainly visible. The anger was not truly anger but hurt. The way the portrait withdrew from the viewer's gaze into its background seemed to indicate the elusiveness, for the artist's mind, of his subject.

But there was something far more important than this. Something not entirely personal. It was the sense that any human being is a mystery not to be fully comprehended. And out of this rose a tenderness, a respect for the incalculable value of a single human life.

Sally sat down on a chair. She was suddenly engrossed, enveloped in her own thoughts. "I like it," she said after several minutes, surprised at her own turn of mind. David was standing expectantly beside her.

"You do?"

"Yes, even if it is of me." She laughed, a little embarrassed.

"It's not a very good likeness. I was working from memory and imagination. It isn't just about you really. I needed a subject."

"I know that," she said quietly. "David, I would like to come back and photograph it. For the magazine."

"I have a camera and a darkroom," he said. "I make slides all the time to present my work to clients. Also in applying for grants. I'll send you a good shot of it in a few days."

"All right." She stood up. "I think that would be great. You know, I don't really have anything more to say. I've learned so much from just looking at this painting."

"I hope it isn't offensive."

"Not at all. Why should it be?" The look in her eyes was one of deep sympathy and that inevitable warmth.

David felt as if his chest were full of soft, heavy stones.

After she had gone, he mulled things over in his mind. It was very confusing. This woman is not so attractive, he thought. He was comparing her physically with Mimi.

But her eyes make me feel oppressed. No, not oppressed. I'm only oppressed after she leaves. Her eyes make me feel good. Not wanting them to affect me that way is what oppresses me.

This admission of feeling left him in a euphoric mood for awhile, for it was an acknowledgement of something he had avoided. But when doubts once again began to rise in his mind concerning Sally's overall attitude toward him, the euphoria faded. He found her arrogant and judgmental.

But Mimi was different. She was pure sensual delight. And fun to be with. The trouble was that she had left abruptly that morning three weeks before and he hadn't seen her since.

Well, what did it matter? All women were trouble. He set to work upon a commission.

It was to be, in effect, a big, tavern style painting for the lobby of a high-rise office building. Tavern style. Realism to the point of falseness of perception. It would be an exquisitely balanced blend of aesthetic baldness and commercial schlock. It can't help, he thought, but please public taste and uphold the pride and self-esteem of the business community. As for the building it was to occupy, a stock brokerage was located on the lower floors. The upper ones were leased out to other businesses.

As he went about the mechanical labor of preparing both canvas and palette for the crude assault that would insure timely payment of his food and liquor bills, he wondered if this bitterness he felt ever got into his work.

* * *

Sally went home sadly disappointed in her triumph. She hadn't proven anything to herself. That devilish man can paint! she thought. Why does it matter to me so much? Oh, it isn't just the paintings. It's the painter. Admit it to yourself. My God, is there no peace of mind in this world? And what have I done anyway? I've made matters so complicated you couldn't settle them into order with a cement mixer.

Upon entering her apartment, she found Mimi asleep on the couch. Her roommate looked so sweet and innocent, she realized with renewed conviction how much she loved her. It isn't her fault, she told herself, that she's the way she is.

Later in the evening the two sat in the living room, each holding an eight ounce tumbler half filled with red wine. As they chatted in a relaxed manner for the first time in weeks, and the wine went up to wrap each brain in a warm blanket of well-being, the two women became the caring friends they had always been. The subject of David arose. Mimi brought him up.

"How'd it go?" she asked after some inane titillation of feminine humor about those attributes in men which made them most interesting to women, especially to her.

"How'd what go?" The wine was already drawing a curtain over Sally's mental perceptions.

"Your interview with David, silly."

"Oh, did I tell you about that?"

"You said something about going."

"It went well enough."

"Oh."

"It went more than well, I guess, but it's hard to explain."

"I'm sorry. It's okay if you don't want to talk about it." Mimi glanced away. She was becoming self-conscious.

Sally smiled with a wine-induced emotional sweetness in her eyes. "I'm not jealous anymore," she said. "Really I'm not. I understand."

Mimi looked at her friend. The admission of jealousy had taken her by surprise. A darkly intense expression in her big blue eyes registered this fact.

"What's hard to explain is what I saw," Sally went on, ignoring her friend's reaction. In her present condition she was only dimly aware of it. "We didn't really talk much. He showed me something he'd done."

"The portrait."

"Yes."

"It's good, isn't it?"

"Well, it isn't complimentary, but it is very good."

"I thought so." Mimi finished off her glass of wine. She picked up the bottle which was sitting on the coffee table and poured another half glassful.

"You'd better take it easy," Sally said. Her own feeling of tipsiness was sufficient reason to warn her friend.

"I am feeling it, but I don't care. I want to forget everything that's happened in the last few weeks." Mimi leaned forward. "Oh, I'm so sorry, Sally. I didn't know what I was doing. Really, I didn't." She had tears in her eyes.

Sally looked at her friend with tenderness. How could she have been so cold toward her? They were like sisters. "The painting was strange," she said. "I think it was more a portrait of him than me."

"How so?" Mimi asked, having resettled herself in the armchair she was sitting in. She was sipping at her wine, one leg tossed in the usual manner over the arm of the chair. Beneath white cotton shorts, her tanned legs were a soft golden brown, like her face and arms.

"The way it felt," Sally said, struggling to find a way of explaining it. "There was anger and at the same time compassion."

"Okay."

"And there was . . . was a kind of depth, an indefinable energy that kept you . . ."

"From being able to get hold of it?"

"Yes. Something like that. It was elusive. Like a human personality."

"Well, that's true of any good portrait."

"But, what I mean is, do we ever know what we're really all about?"

Mimi took a sip and held it in her mouth, turning the notion over in her mind. But her thoughts seemed now to slosh lazily at the sides of her head. She couldn't get anything centered to take a sound reading of it. "I've had tooooo much wine," she said, laying her head back on the free arm of the chair, her blond hair cascading toward the floor in a glossy, silken mass, like summer rain in sunlight.

David, at this time, was in the temperamental process of throwing his half-finished canvas out the window, Paul Cezanne fashion. He had gone out for awhile and, returning home, had seen the tavern painting in its true light, that is, without consideration of its practical monetary value. It was clearly a piece of trash. So, since the downstairs windows were all painted shut, he had simply opened the front door and delivered it to the birds. They would find it in the morning and no doubt sit on it, altering its composition for the best, as far as he was concerned.

Now he sat brooding in the dark in his studio. There was a tremendous sense of irritation within him: a self-contempt and depression. He was a failure. How could he go on like this? Damn that Sally. She had destroyed the peace and equanimity of his life. He had reached an accord with the world before she came along with her judgments and eyes. He had been able to live with his status as an alcohol-enriched, second-rate painter.

But now he didn't know who he was. His accustomed carelessness in art had suddenly become irksome to him. He would be forced to die a starving, penniless genius in an obscure little garret. Of course, there weren't any garrets. Those were in France. But there were plenty of flophouses on Second or Third Avenue.

He got up and went out. His car had only recently, and with sudden inconvenient finality, given up the ghost, so he caught a bus. Riding it aimlessly downtown and back, he then walked several blocks over to a tavern. Going up to the bar, he sat next to a fat, older woman on a stool. On the other side of her was a small, slender man of about the same age. This man, apparently her companion, was wearing a dark blue fisherman's cap, the kind older, working class men sometimes wear. The place was humid, dark and smelled of beer. It echoed the muggy clink of sloshy minds. David sat nursing his beer, while listening to the conversations around him.

"Suzy," the man in the fisherman's cap said, slurring the heavyset woman's name somewhat in the manner of shoosgee, "honey, I think I'm in love with you. I really do. Right here." He slapped himself on the chest with one hand, while holding a glass with the other, and took a large bite off the foam head of his beer.

The fat woman turned and looked at him. The top of her stool was hidden under her buttocks. "I ought to slap you off your stool for that, Fred," she said grinning. "Getting fresh with me! Humph!" She was obviously pleased.

Fred smiled broadly, setting his glass down and showing several missing teeth. The rest were discolored brown and yellow. He was all love and sensual delight at the moment. He then fell off his stool.

"I should've known!" Suzy said angrily, turning away from him. "I might've figured you was drunk, talking through them damn suds. Drink yer beer, Fred. And shut up!" She drank her own, nearly full glass of beer in two long gulps. Setting the empty glass on the bar and licking her lips, she got up.

By this time Fred was on his feet. As Suzy reached into her purse for a wad of bills, which she laid on the counter, he quickly finished his beer, then stuck out his elbow, offering her his arm. She was apparently paying for his drinks as well as hers. She took him by the arm, and they marched together out of the tavern, holding themselves erect with the dignity of a wedding procession. No one else in the tavern paid any attention to them.

For awhile David mused upon the scene. He concluded that they had gone home together to live happily ever after. However, he had noticed a plain gold band partially buried in the middle of Suzy's pudgy wedding finger, and he didn't think it belonged to Fred.

This amusing spectacle had lightened his spirits somewhat. It had demonstrated what creativity there was in the human heart, both for deceit and enlightenment. One could learn from the self-appointedly cunning, and often clumsy, maneuvers of his fellow creatures, if only to avoid the embarrassment of repeating them.

Then he settled into thoughts about his own little world. What to do with Mimi or Sally? Which to do what with? He got up and left without finishing his beer.

Outside, the night air was cool. A breeze off the sound smelled of salt and seaweed. It felt pleasant to be alive. It was all right to be himself. He walked home, smiling as he passed the unfinished canvas lying on the front lawn of his house. "That'll give the neighbors something to talk about," he remarked. He rather liked the role of mad genius, when he thought about it. He would have to throw a couple more canvases out the door to keep his reputation in good order.

Inside the house he got on the phone and dialed Sally's number.

Mimi answered.

"Hi. This is David."

"Hello," Mimi said.

"Haven't seen you in awhile," he continued, embarrassed.

"It's better that way."

There was a pause.

"Is Sally there?"

"Sure. Let me get her." Mimi left the phone.

David felt hollow inside. His heart was pounding.

"Hello." It was Sally. Her voice was soft.

"This is David Mankiewitz."

"Yes."

"I called to let you know I won't have the portrait after tomorrow."

"Why?" There was concern in Sally's voice.

"Because I'm going to sell it to a stock brokerage company."

"Oh. Well, that's good. People should see your better work, David."

"I'm not going to do any other kind of work," he said.

This announcement made it seem in Sally's heart as if someone had thrown open a window.

Oases

She had prayed for three days. During that time her father had had open heart surgery. On another occasion, during a troubled period early in her marriage, when Sam had taken to heavy drinking and had become quarrelsome and bitter, she had sought solace again in the cool shades, the flickering candle lit silences of the church. Behind those heavy doors, where the noise of the street, the tumult of sunlit and fractious day, was screened from her sight and hearing, her heart could expand. It would bathe the room in its warmth, caress the images of Mary and the saints, follow the progression of the stations of the cross to the silent altar and Jesus.

Outdoors again, after such a period of solace and rejuvenation, she would have a strength she could not explain. But being a woman of strong reason, she would ask herself: how can a building have so much power? Blessed structure though it may be, place where Christ came in his holy mystery to enter the bread and the wine, to give himself again in the sacrifice of infinite love upon the sacred altar, still it was only a building, a place of stone built with men's hands. Nevertheless she always went away filled with quiet and peace. She carried two thousand years of human and spiritual history in her breast, riding home on a bumpy, crowded city bus.

"Scuse me, ma'am." A man in rough clothing stumbled as the bus lurched into motion upon leaving the stop outside her church one afternoon. He swung into the seat beside her with a thump.

Veronica had just sat down beside the window. She stiffened, feeling the peace go out of her like a vapor. The man smelled unwashed and strongly of liquor and had several days growth of beard on his face. Veronica nodded as if to say, that's okay, and edged closer to the window. The man sat for a moment looking at her. He seemed to be appraising the fifty-five year old woman in simple brown dress and matching scarf. This plain woman, who had sought solace in her church during the two great crises of her life and during innumerable other occasions of daily existence, felt suddenly raw and exposed. It vexed her that the peace she had felt could go from her so easily.

The man finally turned and looked straight ahead. The bus lurched along through heavy downtown traffic. Everything was honking, roaring outside. Inside, passengers were like wooden figurines. Veronica felt her heart soften its beat. They rode on in silence for awhile.

At home Veronica chided herself for her fear. The behavior of the stranger on the bus had taken a turn for the worse later in their trip, but he hadn't proved dangerous. Just a little disturbed like others she'd seen. So why was she so timid? She who had sustained her husband in his bouts of unemployment; she who had comforted her father in his final moments when the time for dying had come years after the before mentioned surgery she, as a young girl, had so feared would take him. Others saw her as a very different sort of person from the one she felt she knew herself to be.

At eleven that night Sam was already in bed asleep. Veronica, standing before her dresser, pulled her nightgown over her head. Straightening and smoothing the thin cotton fabric, she felt the fleshiness of her hips and buttocks. They had once been firm and lovely, had felt good to her own touch. Now she wondered if Sam might be inclined to notice younger women. But she had never observed him doing so.

She switched off the light and got into bed. The sheets were cool. Sam moved in his sleep.

"Sam." She needed his touch. Reaching over his hip—he was lying with his back to her—she began stroking him gently. He woke up.

Sam surprised and delighted Veronica with the vigor, the strength and consideration of his lovemaking. It was always a wonder to her how he treasured her body. How he caressed her, then seized her with a hunger that transported both him and her. In thirty-two years they had never had children, but it certainly wasn't for lack of trying.

Lying side by side afterward in the dark, in the tiny bedroom of their small apartment, Sam with one hand against Veronica's hip, the room emptied of both movement and sound, they listened to the wail of a siren wafting in from outside with the warm breeze that sifted through their bedroom window.

"Sam."

"Yes."

"I had the nastiest man sitting next to me on the bus today."

"What'd he do?"

"Nothing. He just smelled awful. And the way he looked me over. Then ..."

"You're a nice looking woman, Veronica."

"Oh, Sam. Maybe I used to be."

"You still are."

They were both growing sleepy. The release of tension from their lovemaking made it seem to Veronica as if her body were already asleep, even though her mind was still awake.

"He started talking to himself. It was like he was having a fight with someone. He threatened to kill this person if he didn't leave him alone!"

"Who?" Sam turned toward her.

"The man sitting next to me on the bus. I tell you, I was frightened. I wanted to get up and go to another seat but I was afraid to move."

"Did he touch you?"

"No."

"You should've gone ahead and moved."

"When I got off the bus, he hardly seemed to notice me brushing past him. He was still arguing with himself, or that imaginary person."

"There're a lot of crazy ones out there."

"I wish it wasn't so." She sighed.

They lapsed into silence. Sam fell asleep. Veronica was about to. She was trying to thank God for the good things in her life, like Sam, counting them deliberately and avoiding unpleasant thoughts, when her mind drifted into the loose, pleasant, disconnected structure of a dream.

Cat and Mouse

A couple in their sixties, they had lived for years in mutual toleration. No one was sure of exactly how or when the physical love had gone out of their marriage. They shared the same bedroom but not the same bed. Sam Weller arose every morning before light and went into town to his job with the railroad. He was a tall, thin, wiry man. Judy, his wife, was heavy and of a commanding, or demanding, demeanor. Perhaps that was the source of their problem. Big women sometimes dominate little men. Judy clearly outweighed her spouse, if she was not of an equal height. But Sam was taciturn rather than timid. Besides, those closest to the couple were of the general opinion that Judy had lost interest in sex during the change of life in her late forties. This, they said, was the bur in the saddle between them.

Sam and Judy had never been able to have children. Perhaps that was the cause of Judy's resignation. What was the use of it now? She had worn herself out with trying when hope was a viable commodity. Now she just rested, cooked and baked wonders in her sunny Virginia kitchen, and ate. She ate and she ate. She knew it was not good for her. She had a bad heart. But the beauty of good cooking is that it is an art that always has an appreciative audience in its maker. Sam ate the good food too, the huge Sunday spread when friends joined them in the large dining room around the big varnished brown table for a repast of several baked meats, mashed potatoes, gravies, corn fresh and sweet from the garden, apple, cherry and pumpkin pies, or homemade breads, cakes and biscuits. But his body burned what he consumed and his only comment was, "Tolerably well done."

Such a comment was a shock for those who had not heard it before. New at the board, they did not know it was repeated every Sunday. They didn't see the smile on Judy's face.

Sam and Judy had a pretty, young niece. She was the daughter of a sister very much younger than Sam. Her parents had been killed in a plane crash when she was seven and that is how she had come to enter the lives of Sam and Judy in a more intimate way. Both of them adored her, though they didn't quite know how to manage her, especially as she entered her teens. She could be moody and sullen, at times rebellious. Still, her occasional fits of temper would pass and she would be quiet and sweet once again. She had lived with her aunt and uncle for seven years and was now fourteen.

There had been four great shocks so far in the life of young Mary. The first was the loss of her parents. The second was the death of the bright yellow canary which sang every morning in its big cage in a corner of the kitchen. She, at age twelve, had found it herself, one foot under the bars of the floor of its cage, its eyes glazed, half shut, its feathers awry like chicken feathers on an old dust mop.

The third shock was the unexpected opening of her body to the fertility of young womanhood. It had come suddenly, following cramps and a little nausea. Sitting on the toilet, she had seen the blood. She kept it secret for several days, awaiting death in grim silence like a martyr, then blurted it forth in tears to Aunt Judy.

Judy laughed joyously and clapped her fat hands about Mary's tear stained cheeks. "Oh, sweetheart, there's nothing to fear. Lord, oh lordy, darling, it's a natural thing! You've become a woman, that's all. That's all, honey. You're a big girl now and the Lord will bless you with children. I know it. I just know it. In due time, when you are older, you will see. Lord bless you, honey."

After Mary went away comforted and instructed in certain feminine matters, Judy sat for some time in the big overstuffed armchair which was especially hers. She sat in the dark in the living room and prayed silently for Mary's happiness.

The arrival of Mary's menstruation was still a recent event. The family of three was gathered in the living room one quiet Saturday evening. Mary was reading a magazine. Sam had a book, one of the hundreds of westerns he'd read for relaxation over the years. Outdoors, lightning cracked and banged. The giant old apple tree swayed in the yard, and beyond it, the rows of grape vines, not yet in full leaf on their carefully cropped old stems, were taking a beating. It was dusk, and dark due to the overcast sky.

The living room was very warm, for it was heated by steam through the walls which grew very hot in places. The steam was made by a boiler in the basement, which had once been fueled by coal but was now converted to oil.

Not all living things were enjoying the rough spring weather. One was a mouse which inhabited the small crawl space at the front of the house under the porch, where the family stored old shoes, galoshes and boots amidst spiders and dust and musty odors. The mouse had a small passageway which led through the floor and wall into the living room. He had been there before and was ardently despised by Judy. She was not afraid of the creature. She simply considered it an embarrassment, a sign of poor housekeeping. She had instructed Sam to set a trap for it or, better yet, put poison in the crawl space. But Sam was concerned the dog might get into the crawl space and eat the poison and didn't see the mouse as much of a problem, so he never set a trap.

Mary saw it first that evening. It was skittering along the wall, a little gray thing in no uncertain hurry. For Judy was holding Sylvester, the family tom cat in her lap. She was sitting in her chair. As the mouse passed alongside her, Judy, who did not appear to notice it till then, set the cat down adjacent to it.

The big gray cat went immediately into action. It caught the mouse, brought it over beside the chair and began chewing on it. Then it put the mouse down, batting it about a little with a paw to show it was still alive; then finally, over the course of twenty or thirty minutes, it ate the mouse, cracking its bones noisily in the room. There had been squeals during the early stages of the massacre.

Mary sat in shock, the magazine on her lap. Throughout the entire performance, she watched in stunned fascination, her face white as death. When it was over she looked at her Aunt Judy, screamed, "I hate you!" and rushed from the room.

"What do you suppose has gotten into that child?" Aunt Judy said, amazed.

"You just used her cat to commit murder in front of her," Sam said, putting his book down.

"Murder?"

"Yes. In her eyes."

"Oh, I never thought of that," Judy exclaimed, putting a hand to her mouth.

Sylvester was licking himself and purring beside the chair.

Boot Camp

"Fall in. Let's go. On the yellow footprints. That's right, girls, the left foot in the left one, the right foot in the right one."

The Marine Drill Instructor walked over to the first row of new recruits. He stepped up to a young man with long, straight, brown hair that hung well past his shoulders. He took a handful of the coarse, lanky, not overly neat hair, pulled it back and whispered in the recruit's ear, "You wipe your ass with this stuff?"

"No sir." The recruit, having already been intimidated by the drill instructors, stared straight ahead.

The Drill Instructor dropped the hair and stepped back a few inches. "There won't be any ladies in my Marine Corps. You understand?" He leaned forward, touching the hard brim of his hat on the bridge of the recruit's nose. Though a little shorter than the recruit, the Drill Instructor's eyes fell directly on his. The recruit tried not to look at him. Looking down at a drill instructor had already produced unpleasant results.

"Yes sir."

"I can't hear you."

"Yes sir!"

"You will wipe your ass with regulation Marine Corps issue paper. You will eat Marine Corps issue chow. You will sleep on a Marine Corps issue rack. And you will only shit when you are told. Do you understand, maggot?" He was shouting so the others could hear.

"Yes sir."

"I can't hear you, maggot."

"Yes sir!"

"I said I can't hear you."

"Y-e-s s-i-r!"

The Drill Instructor stepped back several paces and centered himself in front of the body of recruits. Each recruit was standing on a set of yellow footprints. They were lined up in rows. The San Diego sun shone down hard on the recruit depot and the black macadam of the marching field, or "grinder," as it was usually called. The macadam stank with an odor of hot tar. The Drill Instructor, not a tall man, stood very straight, chest out with appropriate medals and ribbons, fingers curved lightly inward against the red seams of his dress blue uniform trousers, elbows out slightly. His brown Smokey-the-bear cap, with its wide brim, large Marine Corps emblem on the front and black leather strap curved under the close-cropped ball of his head in the back, concealed the upper half of his face now. Only his lips could be seen moving, articulating the words that came loudly and distinctly from his mouth.

"Ladies, you're not Marines now. No dirt bag has ever been called a Marine in my Marine Corps. But I'm going to make Marines out of you. You're going to sweat and bleed. Do you understand?"

"Yes sir." The recruits answered in unison.

"That's right, sweethearts. You're going to strain until you feel your bones crack, until you cry for your mama. But she's not going to be here to wipe the snot off your faces. I am. I am your mother, your brother and your uncle. Do you understand?"

"Yes sir."

"I can't hear you."

"Y-e-s s-i-r!"

"Right face."

The young men in civilian clothing standing on the yellow footprints moved about. Some seemed to know what to do.

"That's right, girls, turn to your right," The Drill Instructor said. "Your other right, stupid."

The Drill Instructor made a snappy left face and began marching, calling cadence. The motley crew stumbled along like an accordion beside him. He seemed not to notice their difficulty.

The young men were taken indoors and given haircuts, shaved to the scalp. Then they were taken to another building and ordered to strip themselves naked. They put everything they owned into carton boxes which were to be shipped back to their families. They were issued green canvas duffel bags, which were called sea bags. These they held open in front of them at chest level as they passed single file in front of bins of military clothing and other items. They stood at attention, eyes straight ahead.

On the other side of each wooden bin was a Marine, hair close-cropped and wearing a clean white tee shirt, issuing the particular item for which he was responsible. It was a stuffy room. The Marine reached into his bin and pulled out, say, a bundle of white boxer shorts sealed in a plastic bag. He took it in his hand and slapped it hard into the face of the recruit standing in front of him. The package fell from the recruit's face into the open sea bag. The recruit stared straight ahead and tried not to flinch. Then he moved to the next bin, where the procedure was repeated with the next item while the recruit behind him received his shorts in the same way.

A few minutes later outside in silent formation, dressed in sloppy wrinkled utility clothes, floppy unstarched caps and new unpolished boots, all of which seemed too big for them, the recruits awaited their Drill Instructor. He came out of the building after the last recruit. He positively shone in the bright sunlight in his starched neatness. Every pleat of his khaki short sleeve shirt was in place. The toes of his shoes were like black mirrors. The brass buckle on his belt reflected the blinding light of the sun. It was very hot outside.

The Drill Instructor shouted his marching commands, and the recruits started their long walk across the burning grinder toward a row of Quonset huts that would be their home. Their sea bags were crammed full and very heavy. Sweat poured from their foreheads and ran down their sides from under their armpits beneath their heavy, olive drab colored utility shirts, which hung over them like blankets. They moved in groaning silence across the hot macadam. The Drill Instructor sang out his marching cadence in the glittering sun.

Simple Pleasures

A woman in her middle sixties hurried along the dark, wet street of the city. It was just after nightfall, snowing a wet snow that didn't stick but which was very cold and damp. There was a light wind which blew it into the folds of one's clothing. The woman shivered in her nearly threadbare beige overcoat and brown scarf. In her arms she clutched a paper sack filled with a loaf of bread and other grocery items. A car turned onto the otherwise empty street ahead of her and its lights glared in her eyes and along the wet pavement. She did not look directly at it.

Inside her inexpensive, ground floor, town house style apartment Isabella Fuentes pushed the front door shut with her hip and switched on the light. The yellow light filled the room with its warmth. The worn green carpet, the tired, incongruous, faded blue furniture seemed to embrace her with a familiar welcome. On the Formica counter, which partially separated the kitchen from the living room/dining room area, were several pieces of unopened mail which she had laid there earlier in the afternoon. One of these was a social security check. She set the grocery bag on the counter, picked up the check, tore it out of the envelope, read the amount printed on it—a ritual she always performed—and laid it back on the counter. Then she put away the groceries she had bought, humming a little tune, and began to prepare a late supper.

"Well, hello, Felicia. You come to mommy? Is it because you love me? No. It is because you want food. Always food." Isabella laughed and picked up the large yellow cat that had been rubbing itself against her legs and meowing. The cat began to purr immediately, seeming not to mind that it was being held awkwardly under one arm while Isabella put away some canned goods with the other. And when Isabella placed it against her breast, it attempted to crawl up and rub itself under her chin. Isabella gave the affectionate animal a hug and set it back on the floor. "I will feed you, little one, when I have fed myself," she said, folding the brown paper sack and putting it into a drawer.

The next morning Isabella awoke and came out into the living room in her housecoat. She was wearing large fuzzy slippers that did not match the housecoat. No problem. They were bargain slippers. A stream of bright sunlight poured in through a break in the cream colored curtains where Felicia sat twitching her tail and chattering her teeth on the window ledge. Outside the window a sound of chirping sparrows could be heard. They were in the bushes that landscaped the apartments. There was a knock at the door and Felicia jumped down from the window.

"Who is it?" Isabella asked. She pulled her housecoat close about her and went to the front door. When she opened it, she saw a young man with longish brown hair. He was a very thin young man with a pointed nose, and he had a sparse mustache and wispy goatee.

"Morning, Isabella," he said. "I hate to remind you of this, but your rent's overdue and you're already a month in arrears. Mr. Martin, the owner..."

Isabella made a face.

"I will pay, I will pay, Leroy. I have my check from yesterday. But I must cash it first. I can only give the month today."

"That'll be okay for now. You know he wants me to evict you. If you could come up with more before the end of the month, it would help. He's been on my back. Wants all his money up front."

"I know. I am waiting for a check from my son. It will come. Then I can pay the rest that I owe."

Leroy left. Isabella fed herself and the cat, let the cat out for the day, and went out herself. It was a beautiful sunlit day. Not a trace of the former night's snow and cold, other than the moist black earth beneath the green, early spring grass in the apartment courtyard. On the bridge Isabella crossed on leaving her apartment she could smell the familiar fumes of the cars below. The bridge passed over a freeway. Isabella felt happy. The mail had come early, and on her way out she had found a letter and the check from her son in her box. Isabella was headed downtown.

There was a large department store in this city which Isabella loved to wander in. She could not afford anything in it except an occasional item from the bargain basement, such as her fuzzy slippers. But the crowds, the glitter of new things surrounding her, seemed to lighten her heart. She took the escalators all the way to the top of the building, which was the sixth floor. There she wandered among the pewter, china and crystal. Then on the fifth floor she passed among the furniture: the rich oaks and maples of tables and bed frames, dressers and chests of drawers. There were overstuffed chairs and lovely patterned couches. Blues and greens. Silver filigree and a deep wine. There was a certain odor among the pieces of furniture. It was pungent with the smell of new fabrics, varnished wood that was polished. On the walls were a few original paintings and many prints. Most of both kinds were in bad taste, and they were housed in expensive, generally excessively ornate brass or wooden frames. For these were what the store really wanted to sell, not the paintings or prints inside them. But Isabella knew little about art. It was the atmosphere of rich woods and newness of metals, glass, marble and fabrics that pleased her.

On the fourth floor was women's apparel. There were always young and middle aged women here, intensely preoccupied with the business of making themselves look affluent with as little expenditure as possible. Many of the younger women looked out through small apertures of blue eye shadow, and the middle-aged matrons labored methodically under layers of rouge, powder and grease. It was a rich carnival of life for Isabella. She reveled in its sameness and variety, its predictability and surprise. She wandered about in a happy delirium.

And so it went, until Isabella came again to the ground floor where she passed between counters piled high with both expensive and inexpensive costume jewelry, with perfumes, powders, hose, ladies gloves, ladies handbags, etc. This floor was always the most crowded. Absolutely packed on Saturday afternoons, which this was. There were young women everywhere, crowded against the counters, choking the aisles, ready to sacrifice hours of their time and energy to the careful business of adding minute increments of sexual enhancement to their persons—their faces, their bodies, even their odors.

Then Isabella passed from the store to the street and wandered slowly home. The day was warm. Strange how the weather vacillated! She unbuttoned her coat. She took off her scarf and stuffed it into her pocket. Her shining black hair streaked with ropes of gray fell to her shoulders. Because her hair was coarse and had not begun to show gray until she was well into her fifties, it made her look striking. People sometimes still turned to notice, poor and old as she was. Isabella never felt anything at such times but a sense of joy at the passing panorama of life. At being an observing part of it. She never noticed that she too was being observed. This was why she continued living in the busy city.

Dying

Madeline was ill. She had been sick for some time but had refused to see a doctor. When she finally did, he discovered a tumor, and it was removed. Six months later she was back. They hadn't gotten it all, and the cancer had metastasized. She had a few months left on earth.

Madeline, only thirty-six years old, hadn't thought much about eternal things. She wasn't a philosopher, and she still considered herself young and attractive, which she certainly was. She had always assumed there was plenty of time.

Now it was different. Everything was different. Her two divorces, for instance, had produced little more than bitterness. That was certainly a waste. And many friends of varying quality had come and gone. The ones she still had, she was sure, would not understand this intensely personal business of suddenly becoming mortal. Her two sisters now lived with their—she presumed—happy families in other parts of the country. She herself would never have children. Her dear father, bless him, had been taken by a heart attack the year before. Her less than dear mother (they quarreled frequently these days) would probably make matters worse if she knew.

Madeline was a school teacher. So, since she felt she had nothing more to teach anyone and the pain medication made her dopey at times, she took an indefinite leave of absence. Chemotherapy was supposed to improve things by prolonging her days. Instead, it made her miserable and bald. So she put a stop to it as well. What were a few extra weeks or months of life if they were all miserable anyway? Actually, with the help of the medication, the progress of the disease wasn't as painful as she feared. She simply grew progressively weaker.

One afternoon Madeline went to the Metropolitan Museum of Art. It was hosting a show of Vincent Van Gogh's work in his final period at the asylum of Saint-Remy and then the last few months at Auvers. The haunting loneliness of many of these works moved her deeply. Van Gogh's mental instability—wasn't it, like her cancer, a sort of eating away at the foundation of his being? *Wheat Field with Crows*, in particular, with its dark sky, threatening black birds, and path going nowhere, expressed the gradual shutting out of light to the soul. All would soon be dark!

But the important thing was that, at the same time, Van Gogh also created work like *The Plain Near Auvers*. It was full of light and the arrhythmic madness of living. The blue and white sky and yellow and green fields fairly crawled with nervous intensity, such as one feels the back of a cat to express when the cat is motionlessly absorbed in the business of observing the movements of a mouse. Such a longing for life!

This was the thing. She felt it herself, as in a moment recently when she was at home alone indoors: It was dark then. The very walls seemed to move in upon her. A little of this, and she found herself physically exhausted, her muscles sore from holding herself both inwardly and outwardly so hard. And how strange this intimate contact with her own body was. The soft sweet feel of her own muscle and flesh there in the intimate darkness. And the smooth inward draw and outward flow of her breath, passing in and out of her lungs like a silk scarf. She loved this dear body and didn't want to ever let it go. The thought of losing it was more than she could bear.

Madeline rushed outdoors that afternoon, the light of the sun blinding her eyes. It was so suddenly intense, it was painful. She could taste it on her tongue, and drank it in.

On one such occasion on another afternoon, for it happened more than once, she was found on her knees on the stoop of her row house. A passer-by wanted to know if she was alright. "Yes. Yes, of course," she responded, shaking herself loose from her orgy of light. She was fairly drunk there on her knees and had been unconscious of how ridiculous she must look. "Just a moment of dizziness," she added, getting up. She would be fine.

Madeline resolved to restrain herself in the future to avoid such embarrassing public displays. She hadn't intended it that way. Back indoors, she asked herself: What does it matter if others think I'm crazy? I'll soon be forgotten in the grave. But it did matter. The opinions of others, casual or otherwise, were always irritatingly and unavoidably important.

One day, after months of indecision about calling her family, Madeline drove out to Long Island. She was very weak and shouldn't have been driving at all. Soon she would be confined to a bed. But a strange desire had taken possession of her. On the spur of the moment, she wanted desperately to go to a bar, any bar, and pick up a man. One last fling of ecstasy. Of course, it was impossible. And equally as absurd. The emptiness that would follow such an act would be horrible. Not to mention the guilt. For Madeline had been brought up to believe such things were wrong.

What then? Why was she here, standing in the middle of an open field sixty miles from New York? There was a stubble of corn on the ground. Nothing more. Finches were in the furrows between the former rows, pecking at what must have been leftover grain. It was fall. The earth was a rusty brown, the sky a wispy blue-gray. There was plenty of light on this cool afternoon, but without a certain intensity. The sky seemed infinitely distant and lacking in firmness of character. A deep sadness began to shadow her heart. Why? she thought. Why do I feel like this? Of course she knew why, but why at this particular moment? Madeline still hadn't told anyone close to her that she was dying. This included her friends. Perhaps that was the problem. She resolved she would make some calls when she got back to town.

Madeline suddenly felt nauseous and weaker. She hated these spells. They came often enough, but that didn't mean she got used to them. This one was worse than usual.

Madeline made it back to her car and sat inside with the doors and windows shut. She was leaning on the steering wheel. What would she do? Could she even drive? She decided she would have to. On her way to the nearest hospital, she prayed. She didn't know if there was a God, but she needed help.

Madeline remembered something about an orderly and a nurse helping her, but that was all. In her mind she saw Van Gogh's painting of the *Wheat Field with Crows* and the one of *The Plain Near Auvers*. Between these was the field she had stood in. These three visions became inextricably mixed. Her heart fluttered between terror, sadness and peace.

Madeline died in a hospital near her mother's home in Massachusetts. She was surrounded by her mother, her two sisters, their husbands and children.

A Simple Life

She lived much of the time in the cool of her house with drawn shades because of a congenital weakness of the heart. She must not overexert herself. Heart transplants were not yet a common thing and she wasn't expected to live very long. Nearing fifty, quiet and contemplative by natural inclination, Deborah Moore did not altogether mind this sort of shut-up confinement. She sat in muted light and wrote novels of an indescribable softness, spinning her yarns with an almost dreamlike sensitivity to the color and texture of sensuous, gently brooding human souls. Her stories were like flowers opening themselves to a sudden, clean incision of light, light which was insight that sought out an odor and sweet nectar of indefinable moral truth.

Such things were possible because Deborah had a love of life and had been very active in her youth. The heart condition wasn't detected until late, so she had loved and drunk the wine of experience to the lees. She had never married. Men took too much from her and left nothing of the poet's sacred wholeness. She couldn't abide this. So, as she grew out of the rush of her twenties, she withdrew into increasingly lengthy periods of shadow and quiet. There, beginning in her middle thirties, she had begun to produce her exotic novels. They drew a small coterie of devoted readers, which did not make her wealthy.

So, when her weakening health became known, it was no major adjustment. She had already dipped her fingers and toes into the swirl of life and felt its pulse like an ache in the morrow of her bones, but she was essentially spirit.

"Good morning, ma'am." Deborah had hired a housekeeper, Alena, and it was she who now addressed her. She came twice a week to do the heavier cleaning and wash.

"Good morning, Alena," Deborah called from her bath. "Please don't open any windows until I'm out of my bath and have dried. It was dreadfully cold the other morning."

"Oh surely, ma'am. I didn't mean to chill you. I won't forget." Alena had a cheerful voice, and Deborah could already hear her bustling about the house, doing her chores. Alena always sang or talked to herself as she worked. This morning there were bits of song broken by a monologue which Deborah couldn't make out.

Deborah smiled and leaned back in her bath. She was submerged to her neck and the back of her head. The water was hot. It pressed between her legs, numbing and awakening her together. She closed her eyes and ran her hands caressingly along her torso and hips. Her skin was soft and smooth. She wondered what domestic adventure was occupying the mind of her favorite housekeeper this morning.

Alena was a grandmother and seemed always to be full of anecdotes about her numerous second generation progeny. They were her life and sole preoccupation outside of work. She spoke constantly of them. It seemed at times to Deborah that they must all be living under their grandmother's roof, like the children of the old woman who lived in a shoe. She had once asked Alena about this.

"Oh, no ma'am!" Alena had assured her, her large brown eyes open in mirthful surprise. "They're good children, God bless them, but I couldn't live with them all at once. They would wear me out. Too much energy, those little ones. Too much life!" When Alena said this last, her eyes were black with intensity. A glow of moisture shone on her broad, bronzed cheekbones. She was filled with pride.

Deborah pulled the stopper and got out of her bath. She stood on a small blue rug for a moment and watched the water run in rivulets from her body. Much of it collected in the dark curled hair beneath her pelvis. She threw a large white towel over her shoulders, drying herself under the arms and breasts, then her rounded hips, now a little too full, and her still slender legs, feet and toes. She wrapped the damp towel around her body, securing it tightly above her breasts. Then she took another, small, blue towel, rubbed her long, gray streaked, chestnut hair vigorously with it and bound it up into a turban. She opened the bathroom door, stepped into the open air of the hallway (the bathroom was like a sauna, the mirrors all steamed up), and from there walked into the living room. Alena was running the vacuum cleaner.

Alena did not see her at first, but when she did, she shut off the vacuum cleaner. Though nearly the same age, Alena looked like a grandmother, with her black, silver streaked hair bound up in a bun behind her head and her brown, cleaning lady pinafore worn over a simple blue cotton dress cinctured at the waist. Deborah did not.

"Tsst," Alena clucked. "I hope you'll forgive me, ma'am, for saying so, but you're such a fine lookin' woman. You should find yourself a good man an' not let such loveliness go to waste."

Deborah laughed. "Well, thank you, Alena. I have known men, and I do not want to be bound by them. Besides, you know I'm not well."

"That's why y'should have someone to care for you. A good strong man with a healthy back and big hands and an even bigger heart." As Alena spoke she made appropriate gestures with her hands, describing the back, hands and heart. Deborah could see that this was to be a very large man indeed, and his heart would fill a steam shovel bucket.

"No thank you," Deborah said smiling. "I have everything I need." She undid the blue towel and let her hair drop over her shoulders. She shook her head to loosen the strands, for her hair had natural curl.

Alena stood silent for a moment, observing this woman whom she honestly felt concern for and troubled herself about. "It is for your writing," she said, dropping her eyes and shaking her head.

"Yes."

"I don't understand it," Alena said, lifting her head and smiling. "Who will ya leave behind to remember you and mourn you?"

"My readers."

"They will care only for the books, not the person."

"It's all I ask."

Alena lowered her head sadly and turned the vacuum cleaner on. Deborah went back into the hall toward her bedroom.

After Deborah had dressed, Alena flooded the house with sunlight and fresh air. Deborah allowed it to soak into her, going about the house in a slip and enjoying it with all her senses. But she could not write under such a physical stimulus. Her mind was less a sharp instrument, at such times, and more like a sponge.

Old Memories

He had fought well in the war, in his own opinion, but he didn't know if it was right. How do you determine such things? If you win, it is right and if you lose, it is wrong, he concluded. And that was the problem. In Vietnam they had lost.

"Hello, Sam."

"Morning, Sam."

"Hey, Sam. It's your turn to make the coffee."

Sam Sacchetti went into the break room of the Veterans Administration Office. It was a tiny room with a bulletin board, a sink, a coffee maker sitting on a counter next to the sink, and one big rectangular, Formica top table surrounded by chairs. He walked up to the counter and took the carafe out of the coffee maker. The opaque, brown, coffee stained glass looked, as usual, like a dirty factory building window. He washed it, scrubbing out the last of the stains with his wet fingers, even scraping the stubborn parts with his fingernails. Then he rinsed it, filled it and put it back into the coffee maker. He opened the Ranchers brand coffee ground container. The rich aroma of the fresh grounds was almost overwhelming and more satisfying, he felt, than the hot coffee itself would be.

At nine a.m. the office opened for business. Sam, who worked as a Veterans Counselor, went to the front desk and called out a name from the list. "Thomas Boyden." Sam was a dark haired, black eyed man with olive skin and a carefully trimmed gray goatee and mustache. He was a little stout in middle age. Following him back to his cubicle was a younger man with his hair still in a short military style cut. He took a seat beside Sam's desk.

"What can I do for you this morning?" Sam's cubicle was along the east wall of the Federal Building on the seventh floor. The sun coming in the window was almost blinding. It blazed in the midst of the red brick interior wall. "Excuse me." Sam got up and adjusted the white Venetian blinds on the window, lowering them halfway, just enough to block the direct rays of sunlight. He sat down again, adjusting his tie over a slight paunch.

"I'm looking for work," the young man said. Sam judged with some satisfaction, from the way the young man held himself, that he must be a Marine. Sam had been a Marine officer himself.

"Recently discharged?"

"Yes sir."

"Let me check your file, Mr. Boyden. Have you been here before?"

"Once." He gave Sam his file number, reaching into his back pocket for his wallet and the card.

Sam brought the file up on his computer screen. The young man was a veteran of the Gulf War. He was an enlisted man, a sergeant at the time of his discharge from active military service. Sam explained several training assistance programs established by the Federal Government for recently discharged veterans and also pointed out that there were unused educational benefits available to him. The young man answered that he wasn't sure he could afford schooling since he was married and had a child on the way. Sam, who was struck by the resemblance of this young fellow to someone he'd once known, explained the Veterans Administration work study program.

He also talked about the possibility of a Federal loan. The young man left, saying he would look into it.

That afternoon Sam left work and drove straight to his home in the suburbs. It was a community of impeccable lawns and similar looking mid-price range houses. His wife, a registered nurse, was already gone. She was working the evening shift this quarter. Sam poured himself a bourbon and water and sat down in the living room. The curtains were drawn and the room was dark. It smelled of leather and furniture oil. "Sylvia's been at it again," he said aloud to himself, smiling. He knew the wood furniture was glowing with warm, natural hues, though he couldn't clearly see it in the unlit room. It was a very comfortable room.

Years had passed since he'd thought much about the war, since he'd let himself think of it. He did not believe it healthy to brood on such things. What was past was best left undisturbed in one's memory. But that young sergeant. He seemed to really epitomize—so erect and careful mannered—so many Marines he had known long ago in that war. His mind drifted, slipping quietly over the years.

His men had just secured a village and they were awaiting orders to move out. It was hot and dusty, muggy, extremely hot, the middle of the afternoon. They had already rounded up all the villagers, questioned and released them. Then almost immediately and mysteriously the villagers had disappeared from sight. Where were they? Where had they gone? Were they inside their small bunkers, the bomb shelters in their huts? The villagers customarily dug these shallow pits into the hard packed dirt floor under their bamboo slat or wooden beds. The young lieutenant and his men were gathered on the village street as he thought this. Suddenly he knew.

"Let's get out of here. Move out! Quick time! Let's go," he shouted. They had no sooner gotten out into the rice field west of the village when a mortar barrage hit the village itself. The Viet Cong walked their mortars right down the village street. The lieutenant and his men could see the flashes and hear the dull crumping of the mortars. Several huts were damaged. Lieutenant Sacchetti called in artillery over the radio. He and his men were lying down, spread out in the paddy water behind a couple dikes. He had no idea where the Viet Cong were since he and his men weren't receiving any small arms fire, but he guessed the nearest tree line. The paddy water felt warm, insinuating, as it filled their boots and jungle fatigues. Several one five five millimeter howitzer rounds shrieked overhead and blasted the tree line, scattering shards of hot metal and plant debris. The mortar barrage stopped. The Marines investigated the tree line, found nothing, and returned to the village.

The lieutenant and his men were angry. This had been planned. They rounded up the villagers, going into their flimsy palm thatch huts, sometimes knocking in walls in their anger and rush, and rousting them out roughly, shoving them and knocking them about with the butts of their rifles. The villagers were terrified. They were silent in their terror because they thought they would certainly be killed. As they were gathered in a tight group within the circle of heavily armed and angry Marines, an old man, perhaps the village elder, suddenly fell to his knees. Crying out to focus the attention of the Marines, moaning and bowing his head to the ground in front of the lieutenant, the old man begged in Vietnamese that he and his fellow villagers be spared. He swore they had known nothing about the mortar barrage. It was a Viet Cong trick against them as well.

Of course they were all lying, Sam thought, holding his drink as he sat in the comfortable leather arm chair. I don't know why we ever spared them. He finished his drink, got up and refilled it. He sat down again. He could see the old man looking up from the ground, the deeply lined old face with rotten teeth, wispy white goatee, begging, pleading. As the old man straightened on his knees, Sam felt the crunch of his rifle butt hitting the man's face, breaking the few teeth in his mouth. It was like shattering thin ice on a pond. The old man fell over, bleeding into the white dust of the village street. He lay there groaning. The villagers were silent, terrified, their eyes large and sensitive like deer. The Marines were also silent and attentive, their anger subsiding as their lieutenant withdrew from the blow he had dealt.

That had been a long time ago. Nearly thirty years. Sam wondered if he was still remembered in that village. Who and where were the Viet Cong? Were there any left alive? They had seen no evidence of them upon investigating the tree line. What would happen if he, Sam, were to visit that village now? Would they remember this pudgy, balding, suburban, middle-aged man as the angry lieutenant? He didn't suppose he would ever know. Nor was he anxious to find out. The past was best left unrecovered.

The Arrival

Tabitha was a typical American in at least one respect: she measured everything by its dollar value. The progress of a human soul might, in her terms, have been conveniently tabulated upon the keys of a cash register. She was also very fond of polyesters. Pant suits in particular. This identified her as middle-aged in the nineteen seventies, having attained adulthood in the nineteen forties or fifties.

Tabitha's daughter-in-law, Brenda, was of a different sort. She wore mostly light cottons in summer or winter—as little of them as possible during the interval of her courtship with Tabitha's son. For she had early discerned that the only way to break the mother's grip on the son—though Brenda had not met her at the time—was to get herself pregnant by him out of wedlock. Brenda, a quiet, slender, unassuming girl with straight, unattractive, brown hair, but with an iron inner core, found this an easy matter to arrange. For the young man, Lawrence, who was the point of collision between these two women, was a large, affable, affectionate, often unreflective individual who was always in a state of high sexual potency.

Shortly after the wedding and birth of the child, which two events stood in a close relation, Mother came for a visit. She appeared unannounced, and it was Lawrence who opened the door. His mother stood before him with her brown and tan colored, hard, durable Samsonite luggage beside her. She had arrived upon a Saturday afternoon, not wishing to risk a lone encounter with Brenda, whom she hardly knew, having only met her during the hasty event of the wedding.

"Hello, my dear," Tabitha said, brushing past her surprised son and entering the small living room of his two bedroom apartment. "I felt it urgent to come see you and your lovely wife." She neglected to mention the child.

Lawrence dutifully brought in the luggage, setting it just inside the door. He wanted to consider himself happy to see his mother. But he was worried about Brenda. He wasn't sure why.

Brenda came into the room from the adjacent kitchen. She stopped short upon catching sight of the visitor. Her face dropped.

"Hello, daughter," Tabitha said with a cold smile. She moved like a heavy engine toward her daughter-in-law to embrace her, having already embraced her son, who remained mute, like a pillar of salt, in her wake.

"He . . . hello, Mother." Brenda endured the hug of the larger woman.

"As soon as I'm settled, I'll let you know why I've come," Tabitha informed them both with an air of importance, mystery, and, Brenda felt, impending doom.

As Lawrence transported his mother's luggage into the second bedroom, where the baby was asleep, he wondered how his mother had gotten up the winding stairwell to his third floor front door with such heavy suitcases: there were two large ones and a small one. She must've had help, but the evidence had already vanished. Brenda, for her part, wondered why she and Lawrence hadn't rented a one bedroom apartment in the first place.

Several days passed. Lawrence was at work. Mother and daughter-in-law were at home enjoying getting to know each other. This consisted in Tabitha's informing Brenda about all her own past adventures. She seemed particularly fond of describing the half dozen or so men she'd known and loved along the way, one of them—Brenda wasn't sure which—having perhaps inadvertently produced Lawrence. She had divorced them all—those she'd married anyway.

Brenda observed irritably to herself that her mother-in-law seemed to be trying to suggest the transitoriness of the male female relationship. She, Brenda, would have none of this talk, if she could only find a way out of it. But there was no shutting the woman up. And advice—why, this woman knew all there was to know about raising babies. After all, hadn't she raised Lawrence?

Yes, Brenda had certainly taken note of that. Tabitha, in her opinion, might well have taught Lawrence how to stand a little more firmly on his own two feet. He could begin even now to redeem himself by asking his mother to leave. Brenda was desperately fantasizing.

"By the way, dear," Tabitha said that afternoon, quite by means of a sudden off-hand reflection, for she had never clearly revealed her purpose in coming or how long she planned to stay, "just how did you get Lawrence to make you pregnant? It is not how I brought him up to do things. I must say I was shocked when I first heard of it."

Brenda was stunned into red-faced silence. This big woman didn't need a hammer to put a nail in with one stroke. She could do it with her mouth.

"Really, dear, wouldn't it have been better if you'd waited? Did you have to get him in your skirt so quickly because you were afraid he wouldn't marry you?"

"I don't feel this is any of your business," Brenda answered feebly, getting up, though inwardly hot with anger.

"I'm afraid it is, my dear. You see, I'm Lawrence's mother and . . ."

"I don't care who you are." Brenda suddenly screamed, "Get out of my house! Who invited you anyway?" She was retreating toward the kitchen as she said this. Her mother-in-law got up and followed. Brenda felt suffocated in her tiny quarters.

"Listen to me, honey," Tabitha said in a sweeter tone. "I understand that these things happen."

"No you don't. You just want to destroy our marriage." Seeing that she was being followed, Brenda had turned out of the kitchen entrance and moved into the hall toward her bedroom. She was in tears, desperate for a moment's respite.

"I would never attempt such a thing, dearest." Tabitha's tone was still mollifying but insistent. She was still following Brenda.

Brenda came to the first bedroom, which she and her husband occupied. She went in, slammed the door shut, and threw herself across the bed, weeping uncontrollably. Her heart burned within her chest like hot metal.

Tabitha calmly proceeded down the hall to the second bedroom, cleared the dresser which she shared with the baby's things, and packed her bags. She knew she had served her purpose in coming.

Lawrence, when he got home, found his wife still in tears, his mother solemnly awaiting sentence. This was delivered as gently as he could make it: he asked her to leave.

The following day Lawrence took his mother to a bus depot, silently loaded her bags aboard the bus, and sent her broodingly on her way back to the State, several States east, in which she lived. He was as tender as he could be for such a solemn and determined occasion. There were, after all, no other options.

At home Lawrence was patient and gentle with Brenda, calming her nerves, reassuring her in every way he could. It was clear to him that she had not forced him to marry her, he said. He had wanted to marry her from the first. Yes, it was also true his mother had shown a strange lack of affection for the child. "Mothers are odd creatures," he said.

He was not sure he clearly understood anything that had happened.

Autumn Light

Marjorie Williams was a tall thin woman who carried herself very straight. At a distance, looked at from a certain angle in profile and across the bridge of her nose, she was beautiful with her whitening but still reddish, short-cropped hair and hazel-green, intelligent eyes. But up close her wrinkled face and neck clearly showed that she was seventy years old.

"I don't feel seventy," she once told a friend in strictest confidentiality. "I feel like a much younger woman. I don't feel a day over fifty, and I still desire a man." Marjorie had been a widow for eighteen years, and, in truth, she didn't feel a day over twenty.

It was not long after this that Marjorie met Al Giraldi, a second generation Italian American. They went out to dinner a few times, took in some plays at local theaters, and began a torrid romance. Well, torrid in a sense. Al was sixty-eight, after all.

One evening, while lying together on Marjorie's bed, atop her bedspread in her small apartment on Queen Anne Hill in Seattle, where they had been necking for almost an hour, Marjorie asked, "Al, why didn't you ever marry?"

"Just never met the right woman until now," he answered lightheartedly.

"Don't flatter me, Al."

"No, dearest, I'm serious. I never did."

"Then what did you do for sex all those years?"

"What have you done for the last eighteen years? You told me you've had no boyfriends till now."

"I'm asking the questions."

"So am I."

"Al, you're impossible!"

Al returned to kissing her neck. He had previously opened the bodice of her dress, as she was still fully clothed. He slid his hand under the hem of her dress and up her leg.

After several minutes, Al rolled over and sat up. He was naked to the waist, wearing only his underwear. Marjorie was disheveled. She lay on her back for a bit before recovering herself, then sat up, straightening her undergarments and buttoning her dress.

"You're certainly passionate," she said.

"I wasn't able to do anything more."

"I'm not unhappy." She placed a hand suggestively on his knee.

He gallantly kissed her arm. "It wouldn't do any good," he said. "I can't get it together tonight."

"Okay." Marjorie got up off the bed. She went out of the room.

Al pulled his trousers on, but left his shirt off. He still had good muscle tone. He had been a civil engineer and had never been above putting his own back into the work he'd directed in his youth, and had even done this well into middle age.

In the living room Marjorie turned on the stereo. She set the dial to the classical station. Al preferred country western music.

"Don't you ever get tired of that stuff?" he asked, smiling to himself as he approached the stereo stealthily, moving a hand toward the tuning knob.

"Never." Marjorie had gone into the kitchen to scramble up some eggs.

"Mozart," Al muttered grimacing, withdrawing his hand. Marjorie couldn't hear him.

"Mozart!" he repeated loudly.

"Well, change it, if you don't like it."

Al moved the dial to a country western station.

"Turn it down, will you!" Marjorie came in from the kitchen with a plate of steaming eggs in each hand.

Al turned the volume down. "You're the one who set the noise level," he said.

"It's after midnight."

"The young must sleep," Al added sardonically.

"They have to get up and go to work."

Al and Marjorie ate their eggs at the coffee table. They drank cold apple juice.

In the morning Al woke up on the couch. It had been folded out to make a bed. Al never slept all night in the same bed with Marjorie when he stayed over. She couldn't bear his snoring. And he still sometimes had war related nightmares. He had fought with the Forty-fifth Division in their desperate stand against a German counteroffensive on the cold, damp, bloody, sand dunes at Anzio in the winter of forty-four, not far from his grandparents' home.

Today they were going to walk down to the Seattle Center. There was an international food fair in progress. They would sample the rich variety, then ascend the Space Needle for less exotic but more scenic fare. They could see the whole city, as well as Puget Sound, from the big windows of the revolving restaurant. Five hundred feet up, they could better see Mount Rainier, the Cascades to the east and the Olympic Mountains to the west.

Marjorie came into the living room in green slacks and a light green, cotton blouse.

"You look ravishing," Al said.

"I'm seventy years old!"

"You've kept a good figure."

"You're not so bad yourself."

Al looked down at his stomach, which was only a little extended. He was a stocky man, still in his underwear. His legs and chest were hairy, and he was a few inches shorter than Marjorie. "I'd better get dressed."

On the way to the Center, the road down Queen Anne Hill was steep. Al felt it in his knees. It hurt now and then. Marjorie, stately and slow, was enjoying the morning breeze because it was a glorious, sunny, fall morning and the sparrows were as tense with joy as little springs. The air was pleasant, thin and cool. The sun was bright on the water of Puget Sound.

"I feel like a young girl," Marjorie said, putting a little spring into her step.

She is radiant, Al thought, glancing over at her. And I feel as hungry and husky as a bear.

They were going to have breakfast when they got to the Center. This day, like every day they were together and still alive, was like an orange or golden leaf in the autumn of the year. It clung to its tiny twig, hanging on with solitary courage until a strong wind should come to whisk it away.

www.ingramcontent.com/pod-product-compliance
Lightning Source LLC
Chambersburg PA
CBHW070019120726

47909CB00003B/1001